Curious George®

AT THE BALLET

Adapted from the Curious George film series
edited by Margret Rey and Alan J. Shalleck

1 9 8 6

Houghton Mifflin Company Boston

Library of Congress Cataloging-in-Publication Data

Curious George at the ballet.

"Adapted from the Curious George film series."
    Summary: George goes to the ballet but his curiosity
interferes with the performance.
    [1. Monkeys—Fiction. 2. Ballet dancing—Fiction]
I. Rey, Margret. II. Shalleck, Alan J. III. Curious
George at the ballet (Motion picture) IV. Title.
PZ7.C92127   1986   [E]   86-7469
ISBN 0-395-42477-1   RNF
ISBN 0-395-42474-7   PAP

Printed in Japan

DNP   10   9   8   7   6   5   4   3   2   1

George was excited. The man with the yellow hat
was taking him to the theater
to see their friend Pedro dance.

3

Inside the theater, all the dancers
were getting ready for the show.

And there was their friend Pedro.
He was wearing short pants
and a shirt with patches all over it.

"We are dancing the story
of Jack and the Beanstalk tonight,
and I'm playing Jack," Pedro said.

"First I will plant these magic beans
and then, when the beanstalk grows,
I'll climb up to the sky."

Suddenly the beanstalk began to rise .

It rose right to the top of the theater!

How did that happen? George was curious.

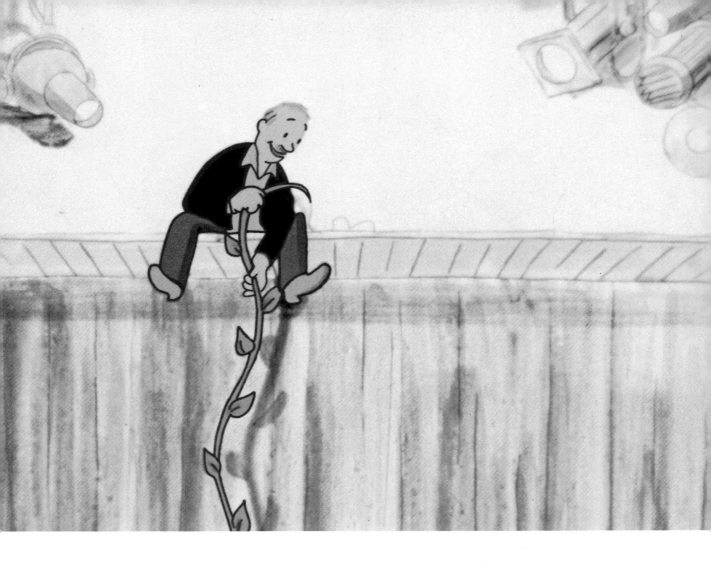

Then he saw a man in a black jacket
at the top of the stage.

"After Pedro plants the magic beans," the man said,
"I pull this wire and the people in the audience
think the beanstalk is really growing."

"Now it's time for you to take your seat, George,"
he said. "The show is about to begin."

13

On the way to his seat,
George saw a big, painted mask.
He was curious.

He put it over his head.
It was so big that it covered him
right to his toes.

It was dark inside the mask.
George couldn't see where he was going,
but he heard people laughing.

George had walked onstage
just as Pedro began to dance!

The people in the audience
were laughing so hard that Pedro had to stop.

"George," he whispered angrily,
"get off the stage. I'm in the middle of my dance!"

George was scared. He pushed off the mask
and ran up the ladder to the top of the stage.

Pedro had started to dance again
and was planting the magic beans.

George watched from the top of the stage.

Then he noticed the man in the black jacket.
The man was in trouble.
The wire from the magic beanstalk had broken!

But George knew what to do.
He put on the man's black jacket so no one would see him,
and leaped to the back of the stage.

How good that George was a monkey!

Quickly, he climbed down the curtain
and grabbed the wire.

George climbed up and handed the wire
back to the man.

The beanstalk grew.
Now Pedro could climb right to the top.

The audience cheered.
"Bravo! Bravo!"

After the curtain came down,
Pedro turned to George.
"You saved the show," he said.

When the curtain went up again,
George took a bow with Pedro.
"Hooray for Pedro!" the audience shouted.

"And hooray for George!"
The man with the yellow hat
clapped the loudest of all.

Dressage
FOR THE
Event Horse

Dressage
FOR THE
Event Horse

FERDI EILBERG
& GILLIAN NEWSUM

The Kenilworth Press

First published in 1993 by
The Kenilworth Press Ltd
Addington
Buckingham
MK18 2JR

British Library Cataloguing in Publication Data
A catalogue record for this book is available from the
British Library

ISBN 1 872082 416

Photographs, including jacket pictures, by Kit Houghton
(with the exception of those on pages 105, 116 and 148)
Line drawings by Gisela Holstein
Dressage tests in Chapter 11 by courtesy of the British
Horse Society
Design by Textype, Cambridge
Typesetting by Textype, Cambridge
Printed and bound by Butler & Tanner Ltd, Frome and
London

CONTENTS

INTRODUCTION

When I first came to England, over ten years ago, I was amazed by the approach to dressage taken by most event riders. They would say to me: 'I've got a competition at the weekend and my horse has upgraded so I have got to do a half-pass. Can I please learn the half-pass now?' Dressage is not like that; it is not a question of teaching horses to do 'fancy' movements. Those movements evolve from progressive training.

Fortunately the last ten years have seen a dramatic change in the attitude towards dressage in Britain, and I think nowadays people are much more aware that dressage is a basic necessity for the success of any event horse; it provides the means of control and also forms the basis from which a rider can develop his horse into the type of athlete he requires.

I think the term 'work on the flat' best expresses how dressage should be perceived by riders, because it says more about the control and gymnastic training undertaken. The word 'dressage' still conveys to some people an image of circus tricks. Work on the flat is rather like work in the gym, or even physiotherapy. A horse that goes well on the flat uses all his muscles well and gives an impression of softness. He will be physically strengthened by the work, and will therefore be able to take much more strain without so much risk of injury during the other disciplines, particularly during the cross-country phase.

By bringing a horse into a state of good physical condition for the work he is expected to do you allow his natural ability to come through and enable him to operate well while remaining under control. This control on the flat is very closely connected to control over show jumps and across country. A gymnastic body will be able to use itself better: on the flat, by producing better balance and paces; over jumps, by using the back correctly; and between cross-country fences, by maintaining better rhythm and control.

Cross-country courses are becoming increasingly technical. You need to be able to tackle obstacles with pinpoint accuracy and to hold a straight line through combinations. For this you must have your horse on the aids and laterally gymnastic. You will also save a lot of time if you are able to go through combinations under control, with the horse's hocks underneath him so that he can land and take off again smoothly. If you have a horse

Mystic Minstrel was one of the first three-day event horses who had excellent quality in all three paces, and his temperament allowed him to produce his best work in a competition atmosphere. He was good enough to compete at international level in pure dressage, and is seen here competing at Goodwood CDI.

on the aids, so that you can stop him with very little effort and release him again easily, he will waste less time and energy.

I saw a good illustration of this point when I watched a horse coming over a cross-country fence after which he had to turn very quickly to jump another obstacle. Because the horse was not soft to turn on the rein he had to be pulled right up (what I call an emergency halt) to enable the rider to turn him onto the new line, and because he was so resistant against being stopped like that he stiffened his front legs, which made him slip, and then he lost his footing and tripped over. Obviously when you are going at a strong pace across country and the heat is on, you cannot expect to have the same control as you do in an arena, but had that horse been more responsive to coming back between hand and leg the tight turn could have been negotiated successfully.

The influence of the dressage test

The dressage test is included in a three-day event to show that the horse is capable of containing himself in a dressage arena and showing obedience to the rider's aids, as well as going fast and boldly across country. It is the first test in a three-day event and it

plays an important role. The ratio of the influence of the dressage to the speed and endurance and show jumping should be 3:12:1 respectively, but nowadays you usually have to be within the first twelve after the dressage to stand a chance of winning an event. The same is true even at novice level, where competition for a place (and thus the opportunity to gain points towards upgrading your horse to intermediate) can be fierce. If you have a handsome lead after the dressage, or are at least up with the leaders, you can pace yourself better across country and may not have to take as many risks as you would if you were trying to catch up.

Rachel Bayliss, the 1983 European Champion, was one of the first British event riders to achieve very good dressage marks. In Mystic Minstrel she was blessed with a horse who had lovely free-flowing paces, coupled with excellent obedience, so she could make the most of his natural movement. I think this horse had a major influence on eventing dressage because, as a result of his outstanding performances, more emphasis was put on good natural paces.

For a long time event horses had tended to be slightly limited in their movement and had performed in a quite different gear from pure dressage horses. If, for example, you had compared a half-pass in an event test to one performed in a pure dressage test you would have found a huge difference in the actual execution of the movement. But Mystic Minstrel had, for an event horse, exceptional ability to move well; he could clearly differen-

Rachel Bayliss with Mystic Minstrel at the European Championships in Frauenfeld, Switzerland, in 1985, when they won the individual gold medal.

Lucinda Green and Regal Realm at the 1984 Olympics in Los Angeles. Regal Realm was capable of doing an obedient test, but because his paces lacked scope for the dressage phase he found it difficult to gain higher marks.

tiate between medium, working and extended paces, and he suddenly began to show up the other horses. Until then, event horses had been judged mostly on their obedience, as it had been accepted that they did not move particularly well. Mystic Minstrel widened the range of expectation of dressage judges in eventing and it no longer became good enough simply to ride an obedient test with a limited horse.

This became all too apparent at the Los Angeles Olympics (1984) with Regal Realm, Lucinda Green's talented little horse. He tried his heart out in the dressage, but just didn't have the mechanics to produce a bigger stride to gain better marks. Although he went brilliantly across country he couldn't make up the gap to the leaders.

It is good that eventing dressage has been opened up in this way and has moved closer to pure dressage. Basically, the two should be judged in the same way because the same technical standards apply, it is just the type of horse that is different. I think it would be a good idea to have eventing dressage judged by pure dressage judges, as long the judges were aware that they were assessing a different kind of horse and would therefore have to adjust to a different picture. Pure dressage judges might be able to give event riders more help in executing the difficult movements (at FEI standard) by providing technical advice in their comments. I feel that, generally, it would be helpful if dressage judges could make more comments about the quality of the way of going, so that competitors can better assess their own progress.

Lucinda Green and Regal Realm at the Los Angeles Olympics in 1984 . The little horse is showing his typical attacking style, powering through the water complex with his ears and eyes firmly fixed on the next obstacle.

Pure dressage vs eventing dressage

The basic training of an event horse is no different to that of a pure dressage horse. The difference comes after the basic training, when a horse begins to specialise. It is rather like comparing a gymnast to a pentathlete; the two must both be in good

Murphy Himself: one of the most powerful three-day event horses there has ever been. A horse that shows a lot of scope and athleticism over a fence will usually have the ability to produce that same athleticism on the flat.

physical condition, but the pentathlete, like the event horse, must spread his talents more widely, so his approach to each discipline is slightly different to the athlete who can concentrate on gymnastics alone.

The dressage for the event horse is mainly to test that the horse is on the basic aids and that he uses himself in the correct way. Because the competition is focused on speed and endurance, the horse is allowed to show himself off in a freer manner. The main difference lies in the transitions: in pure dressage at Grand Prix level you are expected to do transitions from extended trot back to collected trot, back to piaffe, so that you are going from the largest possible reach the horse can make back to the highest possible collection. The event horse is not asked to show such a range of movement.

The pure dressage horse requires a great deal of strength in the hindquarters to take his weight at full collection, whereas the event horse needs to be fitter in his wind and limbs for the galloping and jumping that he is expected to do. Dressage for event horses is all about working paces, which are shown in a slightly longer outline; the horse is forward-going, moving freely and carrying himself well.

There is more time to produce and perfect the collected work in a pure dressage horse because his training is concentrated on learning to work more actively in a smaller space, and he is very highly disciplined. An event horse needs to be as supple and obedient as possible, but in a different range. He has so much other work to do – galloping, fittening work, cross-country schooling etc. – that he is given a different kind of opening-up mentally, which allows him to think forward to a greater extent. For event horses there is life beyond dressage, and they sometimes find it difficult to accept the discipline and confines of the dressage arena. This is something that the rider has to learn to accept and work with.

The German event riders found this to be a problem. Their horses were traditionally stable in the dressage and were good jumpers, but they had not been bred for speed and stamina, and at the three-day event championships they sometimes had prob-

Matthias Baumann with the German-bred Alabaster at the 1992 Olympics. The Germans used to buy quite a lot of their event horses from England and Ireland, but since more Thoroughbred blood has been used in German breeding, a lot of their horses are home bred.

Tiny Clapham's Windjammer was vulnerable to atmosphere. Although in this photograph (taken at the Los Angeles Olympics in 1984) he is looking relaxed and happy, Tiny was having difficulty in keeping him contained and he did not show off his paces to the best advantage.

lems in staying the distance. When the German riders changed to horses with greater stamina and more natural ability across country they found that this type of horse did not respond so well to strong discipline and was therefore less reliable in the dressage. I remember that the Germans went through a period when their dressage at three-day events was not as good as everyone expected it to be, and this was because they needed time to get used to working with the different type of horse they were riding.

When event horses are very fit and working at the top level, their ability to concentrate on the dressage often deteriorates, and this can become a major problem. The movements that they are expected to perform in the FEI tests do not present any difficulty to them; the difficulty lies in getting the horse settled and relaxed enough to contain himself for the duration of the test, yet able to produce enough power for the medium and extended paces.

Tiny Clapham's Windjammer was a horse who relied on being completely relaxed in his mind so that he could perform a good test – good enough for pure dressage when at his best. When he was tense he was completely different and his movement would

*Ginny Leng and Priceless at the 1984 Olympic Games in Los Angeles.
The horse is jumping with such confidence over this big fence that he
obviously trusts his rider and his own jumping ability.*

*King William, ridden by Mary Thomson, is a big horse with a rangey
stride, so he is able to cover the ground at speed without looking hectic,
and he also has the ability to be neat across country. Most important of all,
he is an honest, bold horse, who is prepared to tackle anything.*

be cut down by half. This is unfortunately what happened in Los Angeles at the 1984 Olympics. He did not like the little golf buggies that took people around the grounds, and he lit up every time he saw one. Then, to make matters worse, just as he was entering the arena to do his test it was announced that the American rider Karen Stives had gone into the lead, so the crowd went wild. After that Windjammer just could not settle. For me, as the trainer, it was very difficult to stand and watch, knowing what they were going through and that there was nothing I could do to help. This was something in his nature, not something that could be conditioned out of him.

In essence, the eventer and the pure dressage horse are different types of horse doing different jobs. The understanding of the basics is much the same for both, but the approach to further training and the ultimate aims are different. The pure dressage horse is able to concentrate entirely on his work, so he becomes more settled in his mind and learns to accept the discipline more easily. Generally speaking, the event horse is a lot sharper in type. He is fitter and more alert, and you have to be able to influence his mind if you want to establish a long-lasting relationship that can produce the best possible test.

1

ASSESSING A HORSE

The horse you choose for eventing is unlikely to have the same qualities as a pure dressage horse because the most important consideration for an event horse is his ability, or potential ability, to go across country: he needs to jump well and to be bold. Of course, it also helps if he can move well on the flat (the two are usually related, but not always), but you may have to make some concessions.

An event horse has to fulfil many criteria. You want a horse that is willing to accept the aids and is reasonably obedient, but you also want him to be forward-going and bold. If you have a horse that is totally submissive you might run into problems on the cross-country, because there are bound to be times when you have to improvise, or let the horse improvise, and if he has been too strongly disciplined he may have lost his natural ability to think for himself.

When you go to look at a horse, the first thing you will assess is his conformation and general outlook. Conformation is undoubtedly very important, but there is no guarantee that a horse with excellent conformation will move particularly well, which is why you should never be tempted to buy a horse from a photograph! Obviously if a horse has serious conformation problems – if one foot flies off to the side when he is trotting, or he has a big curb or any other defect that may affect his health over time – you will not want to buy him. What is most important, however, is the mechanical way in which he moves.

To assess a horse's ability to move well I first look for a correct rhythm in all three gaits. The walk should have a clear four-time beat, the trot a clear two-time, and the canter a clear three-time. I look for elasticity of stride and the ability to cover the ground, and I would assess the horse's movement in terms of expression. The natural ability of the horse to engage his hind leg is of great importance as it has a direct influence on the aforementioned qualities. It also affects the horse's natural balance; the way he can carry himself and keep his weight off the forehand.

For an event horse the limbs are particularly important. You should check the condition of the legs carefully and watch how the horse stands, turns and moves his legs. I don't like a horse that looks rather 'soft' overall – soft joints, legs and so on – as this usually means his general constitution is weak and he will be vulnerable when the work becomes more intensive. You want to go for clean, strong-looking limbs, though obviously you have to make allowances for a horse that has done more work.

Next you want to consider the rest of the horse's body: see how the head is set onto the neck and how the neck goes into the withers, and then look at the back and quarters. Don't worry if these aren't perfect. I have seen horses that, from a photograph, would make you think, 'Forget this one', but when they have a saddle on and you see them between a rider's hand and leg, they

Idyll Cruise, a young horse sold at the 1992 British High Performance Sales. This is a nice type of horse with good, harmonious conformation. Although at the moment he is a little too high in the croup, this could level out as he finishes growing.

suddenly look completely different. I have also seen horses with 'perfect' conformation that are absolutely useless. Conformation can be deceiving.

Watch the horse as he is brought out of his stable. I like to see the horse's expression and the way he presents himself. He should have an outlook and expression that impresses me; I don't necessarily mean that he should be beautiful to look at, but he should have something special about him. If possible I like to be able to watch him turned loose in a school to see how he handles himself on his own. The main thing, though, is to see him ridden.

You need to have a very good 'feel' to assess the undeveloped possibilities of a horse, so it is often easier for less experienced riders to buy a horse that has already done some work and perhaps competed in a few novice events. Paces have become increasingly important as the standard of competition has risen, so you want to try to find a horse that moves well. Normally if a

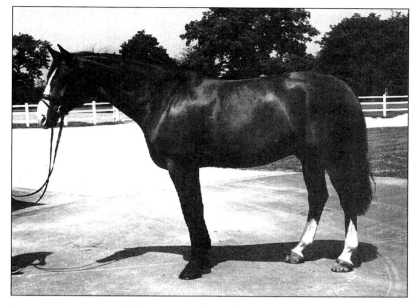

This photograph shows a pure dressage horse. He has good conformation and is particularly strong over his back and quarters, which is important for a dressage horse. This young horse has been in work for a couple of years and has built up the correct muscle structure.

horse can come off the ground nicely over a jump he can also move well on the flat, but there are exceptions. You may find that the horse is very clever and handles himself well over jumps but is very restricted on the flat. The difficulty there would be to decide if this is caused by the horse's lack of natural ability on the flat or by the way he has been trained and ridden. If a horse is

Charisma, Mark Todd's dual Olympic gold medal winner, is a compact and powerful little horse.

Charisma showing his ability while in action at Badminton. In this photograph you can see how well he could move through himself, with a good length of stride while maintaining his balance. He is performing the medium trot circle in the former FEI test, which was one of the most dreaded movements from the riders' point of view because it put such a demand on the horse's paces and balance.

Fearliath Mor looking confident and relaxed as he tackles the Normandy Bank at Badminton. He and Lorna Clarke both had a very determined approach to their cross-country performances.

very natural over a fence, then I would be inclined to believe that his problem on the flat is one of training, because as long as he can use his back well and operate athletically over a fence, then you can usually bring out the same kind of ability on the flat with good training.

Unfortunately, there are no fixed guidelines, and you do get some horses who are very athletic over a jump but are limited on the flat by their movement or temperament. Lorna Clarke's Fearliath Mor is one example. He was brilliant across country but found flatwork difficult because his temperament interfered. Initially he just did not want to be told, but continued training did a great deal to improve his attitude to dressage.

When assessing a horse you need to watch him over some jumps to see how he handles himself. I don't mind with a young horse if he spooks a bit or jumps slightly awkwardly – that would just show that he is alert to what is going on and is prepared to adjust himself. The main thing is to see how the horse copes with leaving the ground and landing, and how he uses himself by curving over the jump. As you watch the horse you will get a feel of how athletic he is, but if you are not very experi-

Fearliath Mor and Lorna Clarke performing their dressage at the European Championships at Burghley in 1989, where they won a team gold medal and the individual bronze medal. Fearliath Mor is well contained, having overcome his initial difficulties on the flat.

King William looking fit and well. He has a prominent wither and a strong, well-angled shoulder. In this picture he looks a bit straight in the hind leg, but when moving this does not appear to be a problem. He has a nice big eye with an honest expression.

enced it is worth having someone else with you to help assess him. You can see a lot from the ground if you are quite knowledgeable, but most people find it easier to assess a horse when they are riding him. When you jump the horse yourself you will get a feel of how powerful he is, how he comes off the ground and how well he takes you with him. When some horses take off, you get the impression that if you hadn't jumped they probably wouldn't have jumped either!

When you canter the horse you can get an idea of how well he moves over the ground at speed. If he appears to move effortlessly he is more likely to be able to make the time on the cross-country. Some horses cover the ground more easily than others, but things can be improved with training. If a horse accepts his training on the flat – using himself with the aids instead of against them – this will help to make him quicker across country.

It is important to feel that the horse is not only capable of doing the things you ask but also wants to do them. There is nothing worse than training a horse who spends most of his time trying to avoid doing what he is being asked to do. Conformation and natural ability are important, but you need a horse with the right attitude if you want to make the best of his talents.

To know a horse well you need to work him for six to eight weeks. When you try out a horse with a view to purchasing him you may ride him only once, or perhaps twice, which doesn't give you the chance to make a true assessment of his character. At the time of choosing a horse you must try to assess his obedience towards you. He might not be obedient to things he does not know or understand, but he should not object to being told. Without a reasonable level of obedience it will be difficult to achieve consistency from the horse. You need to feel that the horse has the type of character and temperament that you can handle well.

When I try a young horse I like to sense that he is open to learning and that I am able to influence him. If he gets things wrong it doesn't matter, as long as he is willing to learn. Some horses may go quite sweetly as long as you do not have to tell them anything, but the moment you ask something from them they change completely, and instead of giving more they give less. A horse that suddenly turns on his rider's will and resists, and does not want to listen, can be very difficult. Although systematic training will improve a horse's attitude to his work and

King William in action at Badminton 1991, which he and Mary Thomson won the following year. You can see how well the horse uses himself and is on the rider's aids. He is doing the 10m circle left in trot, and is looking very soft through his bend and willing to engage his inside hind leg to stay in balance.

Mark Phillips' successful eventer, Distinctive. He has a particularly strong shoulder and well-muscled neck, and although he is not a pure thoroughbred (he is by Don Carlos out of a half-bred mare) he still had the speed and stamina to make a top-class event horse. He was also capable of performing well in dressage because he was a free-moving, supple horse with the right sort of temperament.

improve the understanding between horse and rider, it helps if there is some empathy there at the start.

I am not particularly worried about a horse that loses concentration or lacks a little confidence, because I feel that I can help to improve this and give the horse what he may lack in himself. The problem with buying a 'green' horse which has only just been backed is that it is difficult to assess the courage he might display later on when it comes to jumping across country. You will need to look for signs that tell you he will not be chicken-hearted. A simple thing like walking the horse through a puddle may help to give you an indication. Some horses may appear frightened of something new, but once they know what to do they gain confidence and become braver and braver as time goes on. If the horse spooks, you must decide whether this is something he will learn to overcome or something that will stay with him.

From experience I have found that geldings are more likely to have the kind of temperament and consistency that makes a better competition horse, but basically I am interested in a good horse, and if I came across a very good mare I would not be put off. You should be open about this. What a mare might lack in consistency she may make up for in quality and natural ability.

Similarly with breeding. This obviously becomes more important the more advanced you get, as the horses do need the speed and stamina at higher levels, but an eventer needn't necessarily be thoroughbred. Some cross-breds can have a tremendous will and heart which make up for any shortcomings in their pedigree. Their attitude to the job is the important thing.

On size, my preference would be for a slightly smaller horse who is athletic and able to use himself well rather than a great big horse. Cross-country riding is no longer just a question of being able to gallop and take big leaps over fences. The courses have become much more technical, with difficult combination fences, and a smaller, sharp horse is usually able to react more quickly and get himself out of trouble. As long as he has good jumping ability he will be able to handle the big fences well enough.

You must also consider a horse in relation to your own ability. Even if you have high ambitions, your must start off with the right horse for your level at the time. If a novice rider buys a horse capable of going on to international events, by the time that rider has raised his standard to international level the horse will probably be past his best. Although the horse will have served the rider well, his own ability will have been restricted. You have to be true to yourself; be realistic. You might like a horse very much, but you must ask yourself if you can really cope with him, otherwise you are not going to do yourself or the horse any good.

Glenburnie, winner of the European Championships at Punchestown in 1991 with Ian Stark. This horse is by Precipice Wood and was bred for 'chasing. He has a real tough body made for performance.

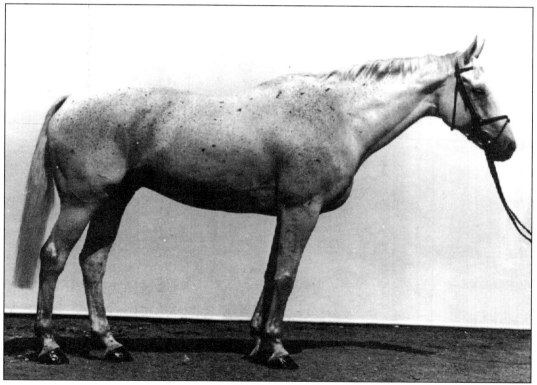

Master Craftsman, Ginny Leng's 1989 European Championship winner, is a classically bred horse by Master Spiritus. He is big and powerful with a strong shoulder, and it strikes me from this photograph that he is very confident in himself.

Everyone has his or her own ideas on what to look for in an event horse, and although you want to stay as close as possible to those ideals, you are unlikely to find the perfect horse. The important thing is to choose a horse whose problems are ones you feel you can deal with, so that you can develop a good relationship. It is the partnership that counts in the end. You can have a good rider and a good horse but if the partnership is not right they will not succeed.

2

Early Training

Influencing the horse's attitude

A rider begins to influence the training of his horse the moment he first walks up to him and handles him. From the very start the rider should try to gain the horse's respect/confidence and make it clear to the horse what is expected of him. This applies at all times, whether it be in the stable, on the lunge or under saddle. Every small thing counts, from picking out the horse's feet to taking him out of his box, because all the time the horse is forming an opinion of you, assessing your ability to tell him what to do, and gauging how much it matters to you what he does and how he does it. Similarly, from that early stage you will be assessing the horse's character, so that you become sensitive to anything he does – or even thinks about – and notice small problems before they become serious.

You need to be constructive, clear and consistent. It is pointless to correct something one moment and the next moment to ignore it. Most horses are naturally insecure, and while they must be allowed to build up confidence, it is equally important to establish some basic rules which, once accepted, will form the foundation of a healthy pupil/teacher relationship. While I personally encourage a horse to work with me on a 50/50 basis, it must be understood that the horse cannot be allowed to dominate, otherwise the learning process stops. Once the horse dominates you he will take nothing from you, and you are wasting your time.

It is therefore important that you learn to do things with authority. Think ahead, and try to do the right thing at the right time, because everything you do with the horse affects the way he builds up his attitude to work, and he learns either to organise and discipline himself and to work with you, or to evade you, and become difficult and push you around. The horse must be given an indication quite early on as to what he can and cannot get away with.

The rider must always be sensitive to any evasion creeping in so that it never actually reaches the stage where the horse presents him with a serious problem. Most resistances start in a small way, and if the rider is capable of detecting them there and then, they should be relatively easy to correct.

All horses form an attitude based on experience, so it is important to ensure that a horse has as many good experiences as possible for him to relax and co-operate with the rider. Everything you do should be thought about beforehand. With a young horse in particular you want to avoid a situation where you might be forced to be unnecessarily rough because things have got out of control.

For example, if your horse is nervous about having boots put on his hind legs in the stable, you should have someone holding him at the front, making sure that he stands still while you put the boots on. Don't trust to luck that the horse might stand still long enough for you to quickly whip the boot on, because you could find that you are halfway through the job when the horse moves and then you have to rush to the front end and grab him, and you will probably upset him. And remember, horses don't learn things in one go. You will need to have someone holding him every day until you are sure that he will stand still without assistance.

There is a saying that nails should be made with heads on them to ensure they do not slip through. Whenever possible, give the horse the impression that he might as well forget about running off because it is simply not possible. It should never become a fight over which of you is the stronger, because the horse will win!

Establishing the basics

There are two major purposes to basic dressage training: the first is to give you full control over the horse and the second is to help the horse to develop in the right way. The day-to-day gymnastic work – bends, transitions and so on – is essential from the rider's point of view (to control the horse) and also from the horse's point of view (to develop his muscles correctly and to become more athletic). Taking time to establish the basics thoroughly before moving forward to more advanced training will always pay dividends later.

There are seven main stages in achieving the correct way of going:

1. **Suppleness** – the inter-play of muscles, tendons and joints. The first suppling work begins on the lunge, when the horse is encouraged to carry his head long and low so that he can relax through the back and begin to use his muscles correctly. Later, more suppling work can be done with transitions and bends.

2. **Rhythm** – regularity of the beat in the paces. Most horses have a natural rhythm which will begin to come through on the lunge

once they have found their balance. The establishment of rhythm is an indication that the horse is relaxed and in control of himself.

3. Contact – a steady connection between the horse's mouth and rider's hands. The horse must learn to take up the contact and accept it without resistance or evasion.

4. 'Schwung' (I use the German expression here as there is no equivalent word in the English language) – the transmission of the energy created by the hind legs into forward movement. This can be developed once the horse has learnt to go forward from the rider's leg and seat and has accepted a steady contact.

5. Submission – response to the rider's aids in the control and release of energy. The willingness of the horse to accept the rider's aids is essential if the rider is to improve the horse and develop the horse's full potential.

6. Straightness – correcting the natural crookedness of the horse by bringing the forehand in line with the quarters.

7. Collection – bringing the hind legs more under the centre of gravity to lighten the forehand and elevate the action. Although event horses are not expected to show collection in their dressage tests, the ability to establish a degree of collection in training will be of benefit both in the dressage and the cross-country.

Progress in the first two stages, suppleness and rhythm, starts on the lunge.

Lungeing

Lungeing gives you the opportunity to establish a degree of communication between you and the horse while allowing the horse to move by himself (with no rider). This is the time to get him used to the tack and to teach him to work with you. He must learn to listen to you, take messages from you and start to discipline himself under your control.

I think quite highly of the use of lungeing in training. Its main purpose is to supple the horse and relax him, but later on it can also be helpful with a horse who finds it difficult to work 'through' (i.e. respond to the rider's aids). If you have to push a horse a great deal to make him step forward from his hind legs into your hands (and this can be difficult with a big, strong horse that is determined not to be submissive, as he can set his strength against you), lungeing can be a useful supplement to your ridden work. Rather than nagging the horse and taking too long to achieve the right response, which can have a negative effect on his attitude, you may find he works through more quickly on the lunge.

You always want to be aware of a horse's mental attitude and also of how capable he is of handling himself physically. The two are of course closely related: if a horse is strong and comfortable in his body, he is much more likely to be positive and relaxed in his mind. Similarly, if the mind is relaxed, a horse will let go of his body and work much better.

Lungeing also provides the trainer with a good opportunity to assess a horse's character. Some young horses have very little respect before the rider even gets on. The handler needs to recognise this as a lack of co-operation which can develop into a more serious evasion. Positive, and sometimes firm handling, is needed to correct the problem. With a difficult horse I always take a lot of time to put problems right before I get on, because if you can form a better attitude and achieve some basic discipline from the ground it will be easier to carry that through to your ridden work. If the horse does not respect you on the lunge, or even in the stable, he is unlikely to have any respect for you when you begin riding him.

The horse will always be assessing the handler, so a good relationship is essential. Patience is of the essence. If you expect the horse to discipline himself then he will expect the same of you. If you lose your temper it may release your frustration but your constructive influence on the horse will be lost because your reflexes take over and you stop thinking. You have to make sure that the horse always has a way of finding out exactly what you want and of understanding why you are getting after him. Punishment must be very clear and very short, with a constructive purpose behind it. A horse should always have an alternative: for example, you can say: 'Go this way and I shall leave you alone, but if you try going another way and mess me about I shall not allow it.'

A lot of horses are not particularly intelligent, and basically they need very clear instructions. The more 'black and white' you can make things the better: e.g. that is right/that is wrong; that is possible/that is not possible. Always be consistent and clear, and the horse will become more receptive to you.

Initially the horse will be lunged with the lunge rein attached to a cavesson, but he should still be tacked up in a saddle and bridle. Ensure that the saddle and bridle fit well, and that the bit is the correct size for the horse's mouth. The type of bit used would normally be a thick, loose-ringed snaffle or an eggbutt snaffle, which gives the horse something quite soft to get used to. Some horses are reluctant to accept a metal bit straight away, and may

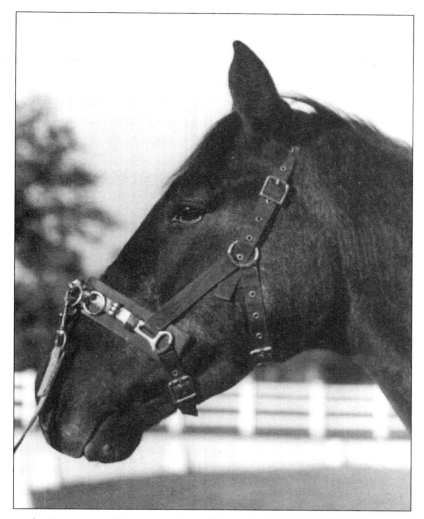

The control that you achieve with a cavesson depends on how well it is fitted. It should sit comfortably on the horse's head, and be firm enough not to slip, but not so tight that it puts pressure on the head. The most common problem with an incorrectly fitted cavesson is that the headpiece slips round and obstructs the eye on the far side (this is most likely to happen with a young horse who may pull quite hard against your hand). The cavesson should be used until the horse is more familiar with the bridle and bit, and has learnt to take some contact.

go better in a rubber-coated snaffle or a rubber snaffle. A bit that the horse finds comfortable is essential for a first (soft) contact.

Care should be taken not to girth up the saddle too tightly to start with, otherwise the horse may tighten himself against it.

I recommend the use of brushing boots all round, particularly with a young horse who will find going round in a circle unnatural and may fling himself about a bit to start with. It is not so bad if the horse is unshod, but he could still cause some damage to his legs, so it is safer to put on boots.

It is best to use a cavesson at first because the horse does not, at this stage, know anything about control from the bit. If he did try to run off, the handler would have no option but to pull on the bit, jabbing the horse in the mouth.

Lungeing in an enclosed space helps to give the horse the idea

A horse tacked up ready for lungeing. Boots should be worn on all four legs to prevent any knocks – a young, unbalanced horse is quite likely to be careless and to damage himself. The side-reins or running reins should be put in place but not attached until the horse has had a chance to walk freely before starting work. You should start off with the running reins quite long, particularly on a young horse, and then shorten them to give more guidance once the horse has warmed up. When the cavesson is fitted over the bridle in this way it is important to make sure it passes inside the cheekpieces to avoid locking the bit in place.

that he should go round rather than straight. If possible, lunge him in a school, using the two sides of a corner and perhaps putting some kind of barrier on the other two sides. If you are in a field you could use straw bales. You want the horse to see that it is pointless to try to run away, so that he will not make the attempt in the first place. At this stage it would be easy for him to discover that he is far stronger than you, so you must control him by making him believe that it is impossible to run off. The horse should feel that you have some kind of magical influence over him which never allows him to come strength to strength with you, so he accepts you as superior even though you are physically weaker.

You should start to lunge on a large circle to establish a good, forward-going attitude. It may be necessary at first to have a helper to guide the horse a little, rather than you having a fight

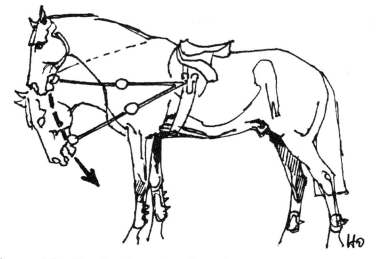

The use of the side-rein helps to introduce a horse to the contact. However, it is not very good for teaching a horse to stretch forward and down because of its fixed radius. If the horse wants to drop his head lower, he has no option but to come behind the vertical and over-bend, which will either make him lean against the bit or withdraw behind it.

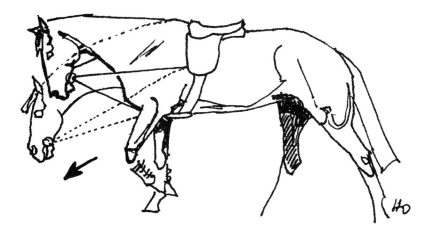

The running rein is used to encourage the horse to stretch forward and down, helping him to supple his back and swing forward through his paces. In contrast to the side-rein, the running rein allows the horse to put his head forward as he lowers it because the reins can move freely through the bit ring. The only restriction on the horse is the movement of the head upwards. Because the connection is not fixed, the running rein also allows the horse a softer contact with the bit.

The horse is swinging nicely forward on the lunge and taking a steady contact with a good outline for a young horse. Note that the lunge rein is now fitted through the inside ring of the bit, over the top of the head and into the outside ring.

with him. A difficult horse may try to stop and turn round, or rush off, so a helper could give the horse guidance by leading him around the lunge circle. He should do this by moving up the lunge line away from you towards the horse.

Once the horse is going freely forward on the lunge and is used to the saddle and bridle you can introduce a guiding rein. This has two purposes: first, to give the handler more control, and secondly to channel the horse's head down so that he soon begins to feel comfortable in what he is doing. Thus, rather than allowing the horse to run around on the lunge with his head all over the place and making things difficult for himself, you can give him some guidelines (running reins or side-reins) to restrict the head coming up.

Personally, I prefer to use running reins at this stage because they allow the horse to stretch his head out in front once he has decided to come down. At first the horse may be reluctant to stretch down, but when he does, side-reins can restrict his head carriage because of their fixed radius, and, particularly on a horse with a sensitive mouth, they may cause him to back off from the contact and over-bend. You want a young horse to bring his head down but in a reaching-out way, with his nose forward.

In this picture we can see that if the horse wanted to stretch down the side-rein would restrict the forward action of the nose and would quickly make the horse come behind the vertical.

With running reins the horse has the freedom to put his nose forward as he stretches down. The lunge line should have a little more contact to avoid being dragged on the ground.

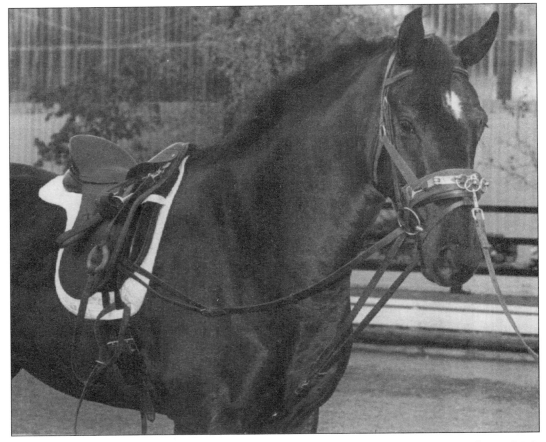

This photograph shows the type of rein I like to use. It is fitted to the girth, comes up between the legs in one piece then splits and passes through the rings of the bit before returning to the girth straps. It has a buckle at the chest and another on the side length so that each rein can be accurately adjusted.

Then he is able to stretch and loosen his back muscles, which allows him to co-ordinate his movements with a relaxed back, improving the rhythm of his natural paces and suppleness in general. When he begins to work like this he will gradually gain more strength in his back, which is a crucial development, because the correct use of the back will affect all his future work.

I have a running rein specially designed for lungeing. It comes between the legs from the girth, splits, goes through the rings of the bit and then back to buckles on the side of the girth or the saddle. The loop through the bit will stop the horse from lifting his head up, but as the head comes down, the reins can run through the rings of the bit so that the horse has the flexibility to put his nose out. With a young horse you should start with a generous length of rein anyway, just enough to guide his head into a position that will make him feel comfortable and help him to concentrate on what he is doing.

Once the horse is used to the bridle and bit, and has learnt what a contact is, then the lunge rein can be fastened to the bit for a more direct contact. I attach the lunge to both rings of the bit

One way of attaching the lunge rein to the bridle of a young horse is to use a connecting piece which clips to both rings of the snaffle and has a single ring in the middle for the lunge rein. This ensures a more even contact on the bridle, which is particularly important if the horse is likely to pull against the lunge.

(using a connecting piece) as this method is less disruptive to the horse. If, for example, the lunge rein is attached to the inside ring only, and the horse attempts to break out of the circle, then you will have to pull the bit through his mouth to stop him, which is likely to upset him. With a horse that pulls a lot I might attach the lunge to the outside ring, then take the rein over the top of his head and back down through the inside ring.

The amount of time you spend lungeing a horse depends very much on the horse and his physical and mental abilities. The ideal programme would be to lunge him and then turn him out, either every day or every other day, depending on how full of himself he is. With a horse that is already well matured and ready to do things there is no point in holding him back or leaving him to waste his energy in the field. On the other hand, a horse that is not so well developed may find lungeing every day rather hard work and would be better off left out in the field for a day. You also need to assess how quickly the horse takes things in. If you have a horse that seems a bit stupid you might need to do a little bit every day, even though he is not particularly well developed physically, just because you need to make your point. Whatever happens, don't do more than the horse is physically capable of doing, otherwise you will have a negative effect on his mind.

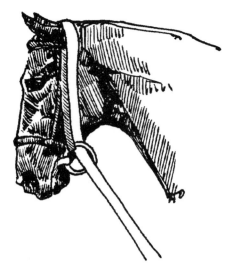

Another method of attaching the lunge rein is to put it through the inside ring of the bit, then over the top of the horse's head and down to the outside ring. This a good way of creating safe but sympathic control over the horse, avoiding any risk of upsetting him in the mouth if he tries to get away.

Suppleness and rhythm in the horse's paces are the main aims on the lunge. Once the horse starts to gain confidence he will be able to let himself go so that he can become more supple. Rhythm is closely related to that. As long as a horse has no natural problems with his rhythm, the moment he becomes supple he will also come into rhythm. However, you should avoid doing a lot of walking on the lunge with reins. A horse should always walk long, and if you start to restrict a young horse who is not confirmed in his rhythm he could easily lose his length of stride and his natural rhythm. Trot is the main pace for working on the lunge, and once the horse has learnt to handle himself well in trot you can introduce a bit of canter and some transitions.

At this stage you will not need to give your horse a lot of extra food. The amount of protein (energy-producing food) you give him will depend on his temperament and the way he responds to his work. It is certainly not a good idea to overdo the protein early on, as a young horse with too much energy is much less likely to be co-operative.

3

BACKING AND RIDING OUT

Only when the horse has accepted his work in a controlled and relaxed manner on the lunge should the rider think of mounting. Remember, each horse is an individual and the training should be adapted accordingly, so there is no point in trying to work to a rigid timetable. You need to be flexible. The important thing is to make sure that you have established each stage before you move onto the next. You need to be quite clear in your own mind what you can expect from a horse at each stage, so that you know when the horse is ready to move on.

If the horse has been responding well on the lunge, then the rider has a good chance of leaning over him and getting on almost straight away. However, a horse thought likely to object should have a low-protein diet and his work increased slightly two or three days beforehand so that he is quiet and more relaxed.

The rider needs to be skilful and well in control of his or her balance to cope with any unexpected reaction from the horse when he is backed. Some horses have a fear of the rider coming up above them. They may be quiet when the rider is mounting, but as soon as the rider sits up straight they take fright because they have never seen the rider above them before. You can prepare for this by standing on something higher beside the horse before you actually back him.

Some horses are hardly bothered by the new weight and soon learn to continue in a relaxed and supple manner. Others may tense and tighten up, and even try to rush off. It is important that the rider does not panic and clamp his legs onto the horse, but just goes 'with' the horse without interfering with him or frightening him. The control still comes from the lunge at this stage.

In a short while the horse should be able to walk quietly round with the rider. The new weight (preferably a light one to start with) will disturb the horse's balance initially, but he should soon learn to adjust. The speed at which he is able to regain his former balance and rhythm will depend to some extent on how strong he is.

Initially you continue to lunge the horse as before, with the horse taking his instructions from the voice and whip of the handler. Then you gradually start switching the controls from the handler to the person sitting on the horse. First of all you must

This sequence of photographs shows a young horse being backed. It is important to think carefully about this stage before you start and to do everything very calmly, because those first experiences have a strong influence on a young horse.

establish the forward movement from the leg. Without proper forward movement, there can be no (correct) contact. The horse should stretch forward into both reins, so that there are the beginnings of a connection to the hand, and he should go nicely away from both legs, thinking freely forward.

Sometimes you find that a young horse takes a while to understand what the leg means, and he tightens up against it so that he becomes reluctant to go freely forward (a stuffy feeling). At this stage, it is better to use a stick rather than be too strong with your legs. A tap behind the leg should make the horse realise that he should go forward.

When the horse has accepted that he must go in front of the leg you can start to offer a more consistent contact. Having given your horse the preparation on the lunge of stretching onto the bit, you can pick up your reins a little more and the horse should automatically reach down to that contact rather than lift his head against it. Once it is clear to the horse that he must go forward from both legs into this contact you will find that you have more

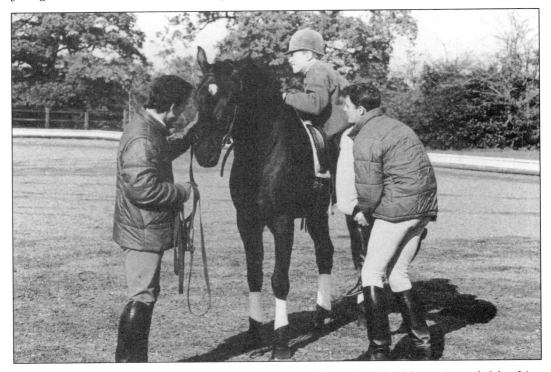

A capable person should hold the horse in front to control him. Considerable tact is needed for this task, as the handler does not want to exacerbate any nervousness in the horse. If necessary, let the horse turn onto a small circle rather than panic and fight against you. A lot of accidents occur because the horse is held too strongly in the rein; fewer problems arise if the horse can go forward if he panics.

The horse has allowed the rider to lean over with all her weight on his back. A short walk at this stage can sometimes help to reduce the horse's tension and allow him to get accustomed to the new weight.

The rider gets into the saddle, but stays light by transferring her weight onto her thighs and hands. It can also be a good idea to keep the upper body fairly low so that the horse does not get a fright from seeing the rider too high above him. The rider should sit up gradually and remain confident and calm whatever happens.

influence on the steering and more control over his balance. However, this may take some time to establish.

When the horse first comes off the lunge, preferably in an indoor school where the rider knows the horse cannot run off, he can be walked and trotted in long, straight lines, allowing him to find his natural stride and balance. A level contact, ensuring that the bit is central in the horse's mouth, should be used to achieve sufficient control of direction and speed.

Some horses have trouble accepting the bit. You need to give the horse plenty of time to become familiar with the bit initially, but if there continues to be a lot of nervous energy in the mouth, and the horse is quite busy with his tongue, he needs to be taught

A drop noseband and loose-ring snaffle are a good combination for a horse that has a tendency to be stiff against the hand and dead in the mouth. The noseband should be quite loose so that the horse is encouraged to move his mouth.

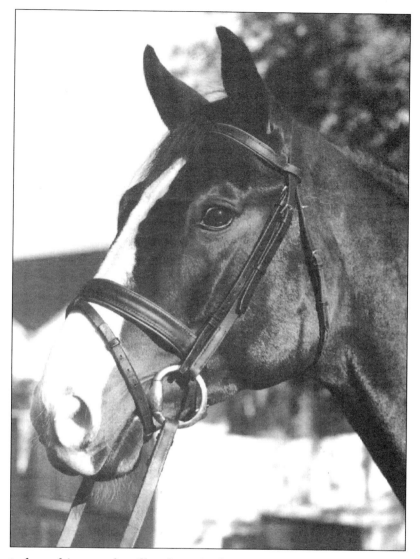

An eggbutt snaffle fitted with a flash noseband. I would use an eggbutt snaffle on horses that are fiddly and fussy in the mouth because the rings are more firmly fixed to the mouthpiece and thus help to keep the bit still, while the flash noseband allows a tighter fit to steady the mouth without interfering with the bit.

to keep his mouth still, otherwise he may learn ways of evading the bit's action, which will be difficult to correct later on. If every time he feels the bit coming down on his tongue and jaw he tries to open his mouth, or pull his tongue away, or cross his jaw, it will be much more difficult to establish a quiet, constant contact.

A correctly fitted noseband will help to train a horse to accept the bit more readily. If it is fitted too loosely, the horse is more likely to fiddle with his bit. It should be tight enough to prevent the horse from crossing his jaw, and in a particularly mouthy horse it may have to be done up more firmly for a while.

I prefer to use the flash type of noseband, which can be fitted firmly while still allowing the bit to remain in the correct position

To create the desire for the horse to stretch forward and down he needs to be asked to go round into the rein and flex his muscles. Although he would be considered over-bent if he were to stay in this position, its temporary use encourages the horse to stretch down as a relief from flexing.

in the horse's mouth without it pinching or pushing up so that the joint hits the roof of the mouth. A mouthy horse will not like a noseband fitted firmly, but it will help him to learn to accept the bit in a quiet manner, and once he does that you can probably ride him in a looser noseband without him trying to open his mouth and resist the contact.

The noseband becomes more influential at the moment in training when you have to increase the contact with your hands (for example, when starting to do half-halts and when pushing to engage the hindquarters). It will help the horse to accept the contact much more readily if he cannot open his mouth and resist against your hands. Acceptance of the bit is such a basic link, and if the horse does not accept it properly you will run into a lot of problems throughout your training.

When the horse comes off the lunge, you must go through a period of establishing and confirming the contact on both reins and making it clearer to the horse what is required. The ideal contact is not a fixed weight in the rider's hands – it varies. I would describe it as however much the rider wants to take at any one time. This can range from a strong hold on both reins to stroking the horse's neck, when the rider, for a brief moment, will give both reins away completely to test the horse's self-carriage.

The horse is starting to stretch down.

As the horse puts his head lower he stretches out further with his nose. Throughout the sequence the horse is on a good, soft contact, taking the bit forward while the rider maintains a connection. If the exercise is done correctly, the horse should increase his swing without altering his speed and rhythm.

Relaxing the back through riding long and down, improving suppleness by introducing bend, finding more rhythm in his natural paces, and going forward from both legs into a contact on both reins form the first major stage of acceptance for the horse. The early establishment of stretching down onto the hand acts as a tension release – rather like pulling the chain on a steam engine – allowing the horse to calm down and relax. It is the key to getting the horse to use himself in the correct manner and it helps him to concentrate. Throughout this period the horse will be developing muscles and growing stronger. It is therefore important that you have the horse working in the correct manner, to make sure that muscle is developed in the right places.

If you watch a young horse being ridden you will be able to see if the neck is nicely stretched down and forward, with the back swinging. Even someone who doesn't know much about riding will immediately see that the horse looks comfortable and happy in what he is doing, whereas if you see a horse going round with its head up in the air, looking as if he is fighting himself, it will give the opposite impression.

The horse's back is the connection between the hind legs and the mouth – a sort of bridge. Any influence from the hind legs has to come over this 'bridge', and if the back is not relaxed and

The horse is now being made to come too round and short, and it would not take long for him to either drop completely behind the bit or bear down on it.

swinging, this influence will be blocked, however much you try to push. There is a close connection between riding from both legs into both reins and stretching the horse long and down: the horse will only feel the desire to stretch fully over his top line if he has been asked to use himself more energetically from the hind legs, over the back and into both reins.

Most of the work with a young horse should be done in trot because it offers forward movement and is the pace in which the young horse can most easily be controlled. Once more control is established, canter work can be introduced on large circles. Walk is best encouraged on a long rein. If a young horse is not capable of walking in a relaxed manner on a long rein when he first comes out of the stable it is better to pick up the reins and start trotting rather than restrict him and interfere with the natural rhythm and freedom of the walk.

Once the rider feels that sufficient control has been established, the horse can be hacked out, preferably with an older horse, to gain more experience in different environments and to be introduced to different situations. This will help you to evaluate how well the first stages of training have been accepted by the horse, and you will learn a lot more about his character and temperament.

As soon as you have sufficient control, it is very good for a young horse to be taken out on rides to broaden his horizons. It is safer to go in the company of at least one other experienced horse.

ABOVE, BELOW AND OPPOSITE: *The training at this stage should be as varied as possible to give a broader basis to the horse's physical development and mental outlook. Jumping over small obstacles and going up and down hills and banks put more demand on his balance and, above all, keeps the horse interested in his work. This is all part of a horse's general education, whether he be aimed at dressage, eventing or show jumping.*

However, if you take a horse out too early, before the basic controls are sufficiently understood, you run the risk of the horse getting away from you and possibly having a bad experience. Some horses will learn to take advantage of the experience, others will be worried by it, so it is better to avoid it happening in the first place. You must feel that you have enough control to deal with any unexpected circumstances.

Once that stage has been reached there is nothing better for a young horse than going out into the countryside, learning to cross uneven ground, encountering new scenes and so on. You can start to introduce poles and little jumps, ride up and down slopes, or over little ditches. It all helps to open the horse's mind and increase his interest. He will also start to learn how to concentrate while other things are going on around him, which will be a valuable asset when you begin competing.

Remember that when a horse is ridden out in different places and confronted with new experiences, he will also be assessing the rider, so always be consistent and positive. When, for example, you come to a large puddle of water and the horse's natural inclination is to go round it (or nowhere near it!) you must decide whether or not you are going to insist on him walking through it. If so, then be prepared for a situation where you are asking the horse to accept your will against his own natural instincts. He

Introducing gridwork over small jumps also helps to improve a horse's physical and mental development.

Adding variations to the work on the lunge is important. For example, changing the site and introducing different pole arrangements help to keep a horse interested. In this photograph the horse is being lunged in a large field with the poles laid out on the circle. This would require good control from the handler to keep the horse on the correct line.

will need to be reassured that the water is not a metre deep and that there is no need to be alarmed by it.

The rider should not become rough with the horse but instead try to give him constructive encouragement. Mentally the horse should say to himself: 'Okay, I would not walk through this by myself, but if you insist I shall give it a go.' Thereby he will learn to trust and respect his rider.

Make sure you do not overwhelm your horse either mentally or physically at this stage. Lungeing should still be used in addition to riding, as the horse's muscles will be quite weak and unable to cope with work every day under saddle. It is also far easier to control a horse on the lunge. Lungeing for ten to fifteen minutes helps the horse to shed excess enthusiasm by himself, making it easier for the rider to establish control when he or she gets on. The horse learns to relax on the lunge and will then be prepared to listen more to the rider's aids.

When riding, I often use polework with young horses because some become bored and rather lazy when being ridden in a school, while others become excitable and need something more to keep them occupied. There should always be a wing to guide the horse into the approach to trotting poles or cross poles because this helps to keep the horse straight and cuts down the influence of the rider's hands. Also, if there is only one exit, the horse soon learns that once he is in the channel he has to go through to the other end to get out.

The poles have been raised slightly off the ground to encourage the horse to flex his joints and to help him to build up strength generally. Because the exercise is quite demanding on the horse's muscles, it should not be prolonged.

I do not mind if the horse is spooky and at his first attempt stops in front of a jump to have a look; that is better than him getting the idea of running past, and it probably avoids an awkward jump. If the horse stops, I let him have a good look and then re-approach it, this time riding more determinedly forward.

Don't let him get away with stopping more than once, otherwise he might get the idea he can stop as often as he likes.

Always try to think through any problems you might have in your horse's training. For example, if your horse is constantly spooking at objects around him in the school and cutting in at the corners, it is no good giving him a kick in the ribs if he is still at the stage when he does not fully understand the aids. Instead, try putting an equally spooky object – a bucket or cone – just to the inside of the circle, so that the horse looks at the new object and moves out into the corners.

4

IMPROVING THE EARLY WORK

Developing impulsion

Having established the first three stages in training – suppleness, rhythm and contact – with the horse using his back correctly, you can begin to develop the impulsion from behind. This puts more energy into the horse's hindquarters which is transmitted over the swinging back and via the contact into forward movement, thereby developing the horse's natural ability to move more expressively. The strides become bigger, more powerful and straighter because, as the horse pulls more forward, he automatically stays more balanced on a line. This is the beginning of *schwung*, which goes on developing throughout the horse's training.

When you start working with more impulsion from behind the horse has to become more submissive, letting you control and release the increased energy. Submission, or the willingness of the horse to accept the rider's aids, is essential if the rider is to improve the horse and develop his full potential. As well as influencing the horse's ability to move well, a rider can also, through the build-up of muscle, improve the horse's physical appearance. However, to make these improvements the rider must be able to put more demands on the horse's balance, and this can be done only if the horse becomes more submissive and willing to comply with those demands.

If a horse is reluctant to go forward from the leg you must use short, sharp aids. Don't leave your leg on him, because a dull horse will assess the strength of your leg against him and then let you work away to no effect. It is a good idea to do plenty of transitions between and within the gaits to keep the horse listening to you, always on the basis that when you say 'Go' you expect him to go. It is important to create the sort of respect that will allow you to be nice to him in the long term and not have to keep nagging at him every second step.

With a nervous horse you do quite the opposite. A nervous horse is basically insecure and he needs a constant contact with your leg to provide him with a back-up. He may not like it initially, and may even become a bit upset, but you must keep your legs gently on his sides (not pushing or annoying him) and he

In early training the horse should be asked for a free walk on a long rein, so that he can show his own natural ability to walk. The rhythm should be in clear four-time, and the horse should cover as much ground as possible in a marching manner. At this stage there is no need to work the horse a great deal in walk; it should be practised only when the horse is relaxed enough to go on a long rein.

In this extended walk the reins are long enough to allow a good stretch of the horse's frame without losing the contact.

This young horse is showing a forward-going working trot, but needs to learn to flex the joints more, and it looks as if the back is not fully supple and swinging.

In this horse's trot much more impulsion is evident, although it is possibly mixed with some tension. The increased flexion of the joints, which is related to the suppleness of the back, is a much better basis from which to develop medium and extended paces.

will soon realise that there is no need to be afraid of the leg. Once a horse accepts your legs and feels you with him, he learns to relax, and then your legs give him a sense of security. From there, you can apply your aids by squeezing the horse, but never actually losing the contact with his sides.

Submission is basically the willingness of the horse to work with you on the aids. It is not a question of forcing a horse to be obedient; he must want to respond. Sometimes a horse with less physical ability, but with a co-operative attitude, will achieve more with good training than a horse who is naturally very talented but finds it difficult to accept the help offered by his rider. Very often, also, a rider will not realise a horse's full potential because he settles for what the horse is prepared to offer him. It is up to the rider to ask questions of his horse to establish where improvement is still possible and necessary.

The correct assessment of the horse by his rider or trainer is vital in determining how much to expect from him. It is very easy to ask for too much and actually push a horse very close to the edge, or even over the edge. Attempting to make the horse do something he is not physically capable of, or is not ready for mentally, can destroy the relationship you have built up, and the horse will start to feel insecure because he has been overfaced in

A well-engaged but relaxed canter. The rider has a steady contact with the rein and a steady seat, allowing the horse to work.

his work. Sometimes you have to be content with a little less than you would like, or could achieve with another horse, and accept that this is all this particular horse is capable of at that time.

You will need to spend time on transitions between the gaits to establish more control in all three paces. The transition from trot to canter is the most difficult. While some horses with natural balance have no problem in finding the correct canter strike-off on both reins, others will have to work more on transitions from trot to walk and walk to halt to establish more control and improve balance before work in canter can be included to any advantage.

A horse can be helped into canter by being bent slightly to the inside. A good place to do this is on a corner, when the horse is more likely to want to strike off on the inside. It is important that the rider does not just pull the horse's head round; the bend must follow through the whole body or the horse will run out through his outside shoulder, offsetting his balance and creating the opposite effect. Again, the bend, like transitions, can be improved by working mainly in trot on turns and large circles.

Straightness

Most horses will be more supple to one side, and in some instances can feel very one-sided. It is important to start influencing this natural crookedness early on, as it will affect not only the bend but also the horse's ability to stride forward straight onto a level contact. The rider must always aim to have a level feel on both reins before he can confidently ask for a bend to the inside. It can be quite tempting for the rider to allow a horse to start bending to his favoured side, because it will already be quite comfortable. But you must first feel that you can ride the horse straight through the middle of your hands and legs, establishing a neutral position from which it is just as easy to turn one way as to turn the other. There will still be a preference, but it will be much easier to achieve equal bend.

To establish this neutral, straight-through position, you should ride your horse forward onto an equal contact on both reins. The more you push forward the more positive you can make this contact, but you have to be very quick and sensitive to level out the pressure in your hands. I compare the feeling with flying a helicopter. In a helicopter you have two controls at your feet and two in your hands, and you have to coordinate all four of them to keep the aircraft steady. When you watch a helicopter it appears to be flying straight through the sky, but inside the pilot is constantly readjusting his controls to level out. With a young horse the same thing applies, and you have to be able to 'feel' what is happening and level the horse out before he goes off-course. If

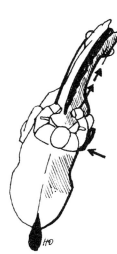

This diagram shows the use of the inside leg and outside rein during turns. As the horse bends, the rider takes over the main connection with his inside leg and outside rein. The inside leg increases the engagement of the horse's inside hind leg, while the outside rein is responsible for controlling the outside shoulder and leading the turn. It should be possible to relax the inside rein.

the horse is always that little bit ahead of you and you are playing 'catch-up', it is difficult to establish the kind of consistency you should be looking for.

The simplest way to find out if you are truly straight is to ride along a line and, if it feels good, ask for some alteration – perhaps ask the horse to go more forward or to turn – and you will soon discover if you are right. Once you feel confident that you have established a neutral position you should start your bend by turning the horse using both reins together; then the moment the horse starts to give in to the bend you can relax the inside rein, keeping the outside rein as the major contact.

With the lightening of the inside rein, the inside leg takes over and increases the connection between the outside rein and inside leg. This helps the horse to engage its inside hind leg more, and take weight off its inside shoulder. The horse's ability to stay consistently connected in this way is of vital importance to his balance on all turns and corners. The improvement of balance will help the horse to maintain rhythm and regularity of the gaits, and the connection between inside leg and outside rein is later responsible for all the positioning in the more advanced movements.

Once you have established this connection it can be used to correct, more specifically, any natural crookedness in the horse, by bringing the shoulder in line with the hindquarters. The shoulder-forward movement is the best way to achieve and

The rider is giving away the contact with the inside rein by moving her left hand forward. When this happens the horse should remain on the inside leg and outside rein and keep the same outline.

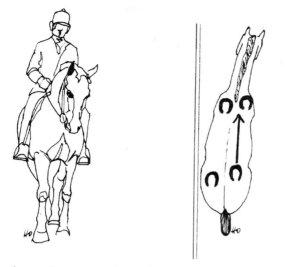

The shoulder-forward movement is used to confirm the inside leg outside rein connection in preparation for the shoulder-in as well as to straighten the horse, particularly in canter. As the horse bends slightly to the outside, his inside hind leg should move in and under. At the same time, the outside shoulder is brought in slightly from the outside rein to create the angle.

A canter on the right rein. The rider is using her inside leg and outside rein to bring the horse's inside hind leg in and under.

maintain straightness, and it prepares the horse for the shoulder-in. The exercise, which is a natural progression from the inside leg/outside rein connection, shows the horse that while he is being asked to bring the shoulder in a little, the engagement of the inside hind leg must be maintained and he should flex his neck to the inside without losing rhythm and fluency in his trot. As the horse is able to move through this exercise more consistently, the degree of angle is increased to the shoulder-in. (The shoulder-in is discussed in more detail in Chapter 10.)

The half-halt

The quality of all your horse's movements depends on the lightness of the forehand. By himself, a horse generally carries two-thirds of his weight on his forehand and one-third on his hindquarters, depending a little on his make and shape. One of the main objectives of flatwork is to teach the horse to reverse this distribution of weight in order to free the shoulder, improve the balance and develop the paces.

The half-halt, used in connection with the forward aids, is the most important and most practised way of improving this weight distribution. Its regular use helps to maintain a good degree of balance in the everyday work and it is invaluable as a preparation for different movements. Before the execution of any movement the rider needs to have established three basic things:

- His horse must be straight and in balance.

- The hind legs should be well engaged with the rider controlling the power.

- The rider must have the horse's full attention.

The half-halt itself can be used in different ways in different circumstances. There are two main criteria – strength and timing. The basis of the movement is a take with both reins followed immediately by a release of the same. As in all situations when riding, the three main aids – seat, legs and hands – are in co-ordination with each other; some have a more passive or supportive function, while others a more active and demanding one.

It is very difficult to explain the use of the half-halt to a rider because there is no fixed pattern as to how much and when it should be used. The rider has to have the theoretical understanding of how the half-halt works, and then develop the feel for using it clearly and constructively in his everyday work. I shall try to explain the movement by slowing down the sequence of

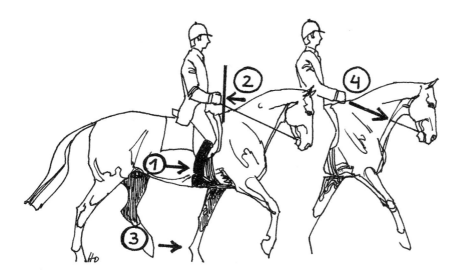

The sequence of events in the half-halt is indicated by the arrows. They occur almost simultaneously.

events which, in reality, happen almost instantaneously.

We know that the horse is naturally a forward-thinking animal. This very often has to be reconfirmed under the rider, but as soon as the horse has accepted the aid to go forward from the leg, the rider needs the rein to control the forward motion. This is already a soft version of a half-halt. In other words, the rein is used to contain the impulsion offered.

The half-halt works in two stages – a take and a give. The hind legs offer more impulsion in response to the rider's legs, which without the half-halt make the horse want to go more forward. This impulsion is met by a take on both reins and is sent back to make the hind legs come more under the weight of the body. Almost at the same time, the reins release to allow the impulsion to stay alive in the hind legs.

The give is as important as the take. If the rider was to hold onto the rein, he would suffocate the impulsion, and the weight would come more and more onto the forehand. The horse has to be backed off with the take and allowed to stay alive with the give.

The feel of the rider will dictate when, how often and how strongly a half-halt has to be given. Most of the time the rider will need to work with a succession of half-halts; one half-halt is not always enough to get the result the rider is looking for, especially before the horse has learnt to be fully submissive in his transitions. In general, shorter half-halts should always be preferred to a longer hold on the rein, so that the horse does not lose impulsion and find himself stuck against his rider's hand.

I like to think of the half-halt as a conversation between your hand (the horse's mouth) and your leg (the horse's hind leg). It is used continuously to improve engagement and self-carriage; to

The horse has been asked to extend but, because the hind legs were not taking enough weight initially, the horse's balance is pushed down onto the forehand.

Now we see the rider working with half-halts to improve the engagement of the hind leg, asking the horse to flex the hind leg more under his body to carry his weight.

The horse is asked to go forward again. This time he is maintaining a much better balance because the hind leg is more under the body allowing the shoulder to stay lighter. This is the correct basis from which to ask the horse for a full extension.

prepare a horse for transitions or a change of direction, and even just to gain the horse's attention. Later on, when the contact is more confirmed and the horse becomes stronger in his hindquarters, the half-halt is constantly used to improve balance.

5

THE RIDER

The ideal, classical seat is what every rider should try to achieve, but very few can sit in an absolutely perfect position on a horse because, like horses, humans are not all the same in stature and physical ability. Whenever you see a sketch showing the correct seat, it shows a rider with an ideal figure. Unfortunately, we don't all conform to this shape!

Clearly we all want to work as closely to the correct position as possible because the classical seat position has been developed to give the rider the greatest possible influence over his horse, but to me the most important thing is that a rider develops a 'feel' for riding. He needs to be able to feel the horse and to influence the horse in the right way. This can be done just as well by somebody who doesn't have an ideal figure.

When teaching, I always concentrate more on a rider's feel and influence than on trying to make him sit perfectly. If you work too hard on the latter, particularly when the rider doesn't have the physical ability to conform exactly to what is expected, you may end up interfering with the rider's natural responses. The important thing is for the rider to develop a deep, relaxed seat so that he can feel his way into a horse's movement. From there he

A good position with the rider sitting deep in the middle of the saddle while the upper body is relaxed but maintains a good posture. The line from the rein into the lower arm could be a little straighter.

The rider is perched forward with the result that her back has hollowed and her weight has come out of the saddle. Although her arm, head and leg positions are still good, once in motion the lower leg would be likely to swing back and the elbows could move behind the line of the upper body.

Now the rider has slumped down in the saddle, collapsing from the waist, which has the effect of reducing the influence of the back. The shoulders have also rounded and, eventually, other problems (such as the elbows coming out or the rider looking down) are likely to develop.

From this angle we can see that the rider has collapsed her left hip, which has the effect of shifting her weight onto the right seatbone. This will influence the horse's balance because he will be sensitive to any adjustments in the rider's weight.

BELOW RIGHT: The lower leg has been pushed too far forward, probably as a result of the rider sitting behind the movement. Once in this position, it is easy to lose contact with the horse through not having a deep seat and hanging on the rein.

FAR RIGHT: The rider now has the lower leg too far back, which is probably because she is carrying too much weight on her thighs and is not pushing from the seatbone.

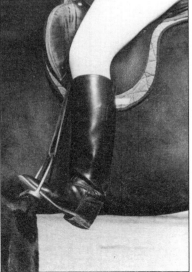

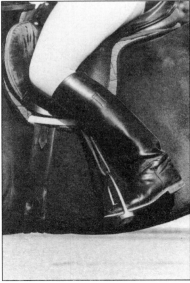

The rider is sitting centrally. It is vital to be in harmony with the horse's body to help him to keep his own balance centred.

LEFT: *The rider is gripping upwards from the knee, which has the effect of pushing her out of the saddle so that she loses the influence of her seat.*

In this picture we can see the rider pushing her weight down into the stirrup but away from the horse so that she is not keeping enough contact with the lower leg. From this position the toes are likely to start turning out.

Here the rider has her leg nicely wrapped around the horse without clamping her leg on him and looking too tight.

puts his legs, hands and head into the correct positions.

We all have to watch ourselves, even those riders who have a good feel and a deep, relaxed seat, to ensure that no faults creep in. These usually start with the extremities of the body – the head, hands, legs and feet. If bad habits develop here then, initially, it is just the overall picture that is affected, but soon the faults will start to interfere with the rider's influence. For example, if the hands are too high, or turning inwards, then the elbows may start to stick out and then the next thing is that the shoulders start to round and the influence of the back is reduced. It is like a chain reaction. You need to put a stop to any bad habits, however small, right at the beginning, and this requires a lot of self-discipline, especially if you ride by yourself.

The amount of tuition you need will depend on how natural you are on a horse and what you are hoping to achieve. Even good riders need a check-up now and then. The main thing is to gain as much practical experience as possible. You can base your riding on theory, but often when you come to put it to the test it doesn't work out the way you expect because 'feel' cannot be learned from a book!

You should aim to develop an independent seat, so that you can operate your legs and hands without having to worry about your own balance. If you cannot do this you will automatically (though perhaps subconsciously) use the hand and leg to steady yourself, so that when you are in a situation where you should actually be lightening the contact you are instead holding onto the rein and clamping your legs against the horse. If you can go with the movement of the horse just from your seat, then you can do what you like with your hands and legs, enabling you to give much clearer aids.

To develop this independent seat it is best to do a lot of work without stirrups, preferably on the lunge where the rider doesn't have to worry about controlling the horse. This will obviously involve some extra help and tuition but it will be well worth it in the long run. Even when you have achieved an independent seat, riding without stirrups every now and then is of great value in maintaining a deep seat.

Mark Todd and Charisma at the Seoul Olympics, where they won their second individual gold medal. Mark maintains a very correct and relaxed seat under the strain of the competition.

6

TOWARDS COMPETITION

Preparing for test riding

There is only a certain amount of training and preparation that you can do at home before it is time to take a horse out and broaden his horizons. Obviously your training at home will continue between outings and competitions, but you need to take your horse away from the home environment sometimes so that he can gain more experience and you can learn more about his temperament and character. This may give you new problems and thus new incentives on what to work on at home. It all helps to prepare him for future competitions, where you will want him to go consistently well. That is what counts in the end: the ability of the horse to produce his best work at a competition, not just at home.

It is often a good idea to take a young, nervous or highly strung horse to two or three shows or events in fairly quick succession to make him realise that they are really not that exciting. If you take him to one competition, and then leave a long gap before going to another, he will probably react in the same way as he did the first time. He may need to go on quite a few outings before he learns to settle and not be so excitable, and the wider the range of activities the better.

When working up to a one-day event your horse will be becoming much fitter than he was in his early schooling, and you will probably find that he starts to react differently to his flatwork. He may become less submissive to the aids, so you must be prepared for these changes and not allow the horse to use his strength and fitness against you to escape from the aids. The horse may need to work for a little longer, and it can be a great help to deal with any extra enthusiasm on the lunge. It is important that you can still handle the horse when he is competition fit.

Obviously you will feel more confident at your first competitions if you know that your horse has been going well at home.

There are all sorts of problems that you may encounter when training your horse, whether he is a youngster or a more experienced horse, and some of these are discussed below and in Chapter 7. However, there is a danger in prescribing specific exercises to deal with specific problems because the exercises can be completely wasted, and possibly do more harm than good, if the rider has not properly established his basic links. For example, there is no point in asking for a shoulder-in when you do not have a good enough contact and your horse is stiff in the back. The exercise will only increase the engagement of the inside hind leg if the horse is using himself in the correct way.

The basic way of going – an acceptance of the aids and of the contact, a supple back and the horse going forward from the leg – is a pre-requisite to using exercises like transitions and shoulder-in to make things even better. If you have a horse that is using himself in the wrong way and his rider is not knowledgeable enough to realise that he is doing the exercises incorrectly, the horse will move further and further from the proper way of going. Usually you find that if a horse has difficulty with any sort of movement you can trace it back to some very basic missing link.

Most problems that arise in novice and intermediate tests are related to the horse's lack of balance. In other words, the horse cannot control his weight in the confines of the small arena and will try to save himself by going on the forehand. Other results of this can be (just to mention a few common shortcomings) irregularity, lack of bend, and resistance through transitions. If a horse is capable of staying balanced in his paces on all the different lines of the dressage arena – circles, diagonals, serpentines, etc. – then he should have no difficulty in performing any kind of movement that has been learnt at home.

A dressage test is often not seen for what it really is. It is just riding around an arena in balance. People talk about a test consisting of movements, and concentrate very hard on a particular movement, such as a 20-metre circle, when really they should be concentrating on the horse's overall balance and rhythm. Even at the highest levels in pure dressage, although the difficulty of movements is of course increased, you still have to ride through a corner, ride down the centre line, turn onto the diagonal, ride circles and so on. I have come across advanced horses who can do all the fancy movements, but who are not really in balance, and if you rode them through a novice test they would still not be in perfect balance even on the simple things.

When preparing for a competition you must practise some arena work with your horse. If you have been riding in a field with plenty of space you may have felt that your horse was in perfect balance, but probably you have subconsciously been going where the horse's balance was going. You don't find out how much in balance the horse really is until you put him into the four corners of an arena. Practice in an arena is as much for your benefit – to find out how well the horse is between your leg and hand – as it is for the horse's, to learn to adjust his balance and gain confidence.

Practising in an arena is an important part of your preparation for a competition.

Put yourself in the horse's position. If he has never been in an arena – especially an indoor school where there is a solid wall – the horse has to know, for his own confidence, that you will turn when you get to the end of the centre line or the diagonal and that you will not run him into the wall. It is a simple thing, but the horse may start to tighten and tense his back, because he is not sure exactly what is going to happen when he arrives at the corner.

The horse also needs to get used to working in a confined space in the open, in other words a dressage arena placed in the middle of a big field, which is what you will be faced with at a novice one-day event. The small white boards are not enough to keep the horse balanced within the boundaries set by the arena, particularly when there are big gaps between the boards! The horse has to allow the rider to balance him between leg and hand and learn through practice to work confidently within the limits of the arena.

Working within an arena demands a high degree of accuracy. Any horse will cut the corners, or come back from the diagonal onto the track too soon, or overshoot the markers, if he gets the impression that it doesn't matter. He will only shape up to your expectations if he feels it matters to you, so you have to make him realise that it is important that he stops at exactly this point or goes properly into the corner. If you have to come down the centre line fifty times in order to hit the marker and stop in the right place, then that is what you must do to make him understand how strongly you feel about it. You cannot tell him in words, so you have to do it until it is right, and when it is right, you must let him know. Consistency and accuracy are essential; it is no good caring about something one day and not the next, otherwise the horse will not know what to expect. Unlike your training at home, where the process is gradual and you don't expect things to be completely right straight away, in a test there can be no allowances: you are either on the right marker or you are not. There is no in-between.

Before riding a test you will need to appreciate the difference between working, medium and extended paces. There is no fixed measure for these because they depend on the range of the individual horse and his ability to move. For some horses a working trot might be what others can do in medium trot. What the judge will want to see, and what you, as a rider, will want to feel, is that the horse is making an effort and is using himself to the best of his ability.

The working trot is a fresh, active trot based on the natural ability of the horse. In the medium trot the horse covers more

A flowing medium trot from Welton Greylag (with Mark Todd). To produce good movement like this the horse must be swinging through his back. Welton Greylag is looking alert but relaxed, and in lovely self-carriage. The rider is sitting well and has maintained a light contact with the horse's mouth.

ground and lengthens the overall frame of his body with the size of his stride, but he should still swing freely through his back and stay very rhythmical. Extended trot increases the reach, covering even more ground and extending the horse's frame further, so that in the ultimate extended trot you get the feel that this is the limit of the horse's capabilities.

People often think that the medium trot should be half as engaged as the extended trot, but this is not so. A horse should always be basically engaged, it is just the length of the stride and frame that changes. In the collected trot, for example, the engagement is more in a carrying capacity. There is less forward action, and the steps should gain more lift off the ground. In the working trot the engagement becomes more forward so that the horse is freer but still nicely off the ground. In medium trot the engagement changes into more pushing and slightly less carrying, and this is further expanded in the extended trot, but the carrying capacity should not be lost otherwise the horse would go more and more onto his forehand. If you over-push a horse in an extended trot he can go forward too much and overpower the front, and then his balance can't cope and he has to break the rhythm. Some horses give the impression of extending extravagantly when they are actually going nowhere. This is because they throw their foreleg out in front of them with a rather showy movement, but the leg comes back down again to meet the ground rather than reaching forward. When this happens the hind legs are not truly engaged and the horse doesn't cover enough ground.

When a horse breaks the rhythm in an extended trot it may be because he is too tense and just wants to run off. Some horses tend to become faster in their rhythm, and this is usually because they are too tight in the back, so the back does not swing. The energy is there, but because it cannot be combined with the swinging back the horse loses the clear rhythm of the diagonal.

This can happen in the medium trot as well. It was particularly noticeable in the old FEI three-day event test in which the medium trot was done on a circle, making the balance more difficult.

To overcome the problem you need to make the horse more confident about using a lot of energy from behind without running away from the leg. What often happens is that a horse remains calm, relaxed and swinging in the back as long as you don't ask for the sort of energy needed in a medium or extended trot. Then when you do ask for more energy the horse starts to worry about it and becomes slightly tense, which impairs his ability to stay swinging. You need to work with transitions within the gait to help the horse use his hind leg more effectively, and this will gradually help him to feel more capable of keeping his balance. If a horse feels that he is struggling he will become tense.

The transitions between working and medium trot are

important because in the test the mark includes the transition, so it is not enough to show a few good strides and then have a resistance against the hands or an interruption in the rhythm on the coming back. That will still hit your score.

When riding a downward transition the rider should be careful not to just pull backward with the rein, as this has the effect of stopping the shoulder while the hind legs are still pushing forward. The physical force from behind will make the horse lower his wither and increase the weight on the forehand. The horse has to learn to come back by engaging his hind legs more under his weight, so that the forehand can stay light as he makes the transition. To do this the horse has to be soft enough in the back so that he can let the half-halt through into the hind legs without stopping up on the shoulder.

When a horse is too heavy on the hand and the rider wants to make a transition from canter to trot, for example, it very easily happens that the horse falls into trot during the preparatory half-halt. So it is important that there is enough self-carriage before a transition is attempted, and that the rider does not just pull back with his hands.

Improving the transitions goes back to the horse's acceptance of the contact. The contact is there to make the connection to the horse's hind legs. When you give the horse a half-halt you should instantly feel that the hind legs are willing to step more forward under the body. A horse that connects well between the rider's leg and hand will feel in one piece and will more easily carry the weight on his hind legs, and it is this which has the most positive influence on the balance.

In your training you are working to improve the connection all the time so that the hind legs come more and more under the horse's weight. You keep a sort of conversation going between you and your horse, with little half-halts, slight changes of pace, and so on, quietly demanding that the horse become a little more expressive, a little more off the ground and uses himself better.

There is a world of difference between working a horse and just exercising one. A wonderful comment I once heard came from an examiner who was asked to remark on a particular rider's ability to influence his horse. His response was: 'Well, quite frankly, when I saw him I thought, "Oh, there is a loose horse with a man on".' That sums up the difference very well!

Developing collection

The dressage tests in eventing, even at international level, ask only for working, medium and extended paces, but it is useful to work towards a degree of collection in training because it will improve the horse's balance and expression, and his way of going. Horses lacking natural movement can develop a bigger stride through learning to collect, and they can gain better balance, giving them the ability to move in a way that would not be possible without the rider's assistance.

Collection basically means that the horse is capable of lowering his hindquarters and taking more weight on them, which then allows him to develop his stride with more freedom and lightness on the forehand. To produce the best possible extended trot from your horse he needs to be able to collect.

Achieving a small degree of collection will also help to improve the horse's other paces and movements. For example, at moments like the transition from canter to halt, if you can put your horse back on his hindquarters for an instant you will have a better halt, with the horse coming off the forehand. If, on the other hand, the horse is in working canter because that is all he can do, and he is not capable of collection in the canter, when you do the transition you will find that the sheer pace will push the horse onto the forehand and make him fall against your hands.

Collection will also affect a horse's ability across country, particularly when you have to make tight turns or be very precise on a line. There are often alternatives at obstacles: one may be a bold, attacking, straight-through route; another might be a longer, often quite tight and twisty route. If you decide that the bold route is too risky you can opt for the alternative without wasting too much time because, provided your horse is capable of some collection, he can come right back to you without losing his rhythm, and he will stay fluent. (Collection is also discussed in Chapter 10.)

The halt

The halt is one of the more basic movements asked for in dressage tests but it is, at the same time, very complex and quite a few marks will depend on it. The halt needs to be taught correctly and should be introduced very early on in the training of the young horse. The horse should learn to stand still while being mounted and dismounted, and while being handled.

The main criterion of the halt is immobility for as long or as short a time as the rider wants. As the horse becomes more balanced in his paces and learns to accept the contact he will automatically become more balanced into the halt. Standing in a balanced way means that the horse distributes his weight equally on all four legs and stands straight and square.

The most common problem that the rider has to deal with in the early stages of training is the lack of submission between

hand and leg as the horse comes into halt. On the last steps before the standstill the horse should engage more and lower the quarters so that he can take the weight off the forehand and come into halt with no effort or resistance against the hand. This is achieved mainly by good use of half-halts in the preparation.

It is very important that the rider assesses the temperament of his horse so that he can deal with individual evasions when working on the halt. Any resistance against the hand usually shows itself in the horse throwing his head up or taking it down behind the vertical, and so blocking the connection to the hind legs. This makes it difficult to actually stop, because the hind legs keep pushing the weight forward against the hand. At the same time the horse is likely to become crooked and, when finally pulled up, will not want to stand still.

Another problem is that the horse withdraws the engagement and forwardness too quickly before the standstill, and uses the halt to get behind the rider's forward aids. This results in the horse going down on the withers and possibly backing off altogether, stepping back in the halt.

Most of the problems can be felt in the preparation and must

Richard Meade and Kilcashel give a nice halt and salute at the World Championships in Luhmühlen, 1982. The horse is not completely square but he looks balanced and relaxed.

be dealt with there and then. The horse must be in front of the forward aids at all times, and the connection between hand and leg (i.e. the horse's mouth and his hind legs) must be accepted and alive. The rider should make it clear to the horse that a solid standstill, in front of the leg and on a still contact, is the basis of a good halt. If the horse stands awkwardly or unbalanced he should be corrected by moving one or two steps forward and then establishing another halt. The same correction is necessary if the horse tries to come behind the leg or becomes unsteady in the contact.

If the horse stands fairly balanced and on the aids, but not quite square, the rider should ask him to move the individual leg or legs forward to support his weight equally by confirming or increasing the forward pull between leg and hand. A clear and constructive correction is required at all times, so as not to upset the basic idea of standing still.

The rein-back

The rein-back plays a very important role in the training of the horse. It is used to test the degree of submission and obedience as well as the suppleness of the horse. It is also a very useful exercise to improve the horse's attention and his lightness of the forehand. If there is no physical problem, every horse should be

A rein-back in competition. The steps look reasonably diagonal and the rider is allowing the horse's back to come up, but the horse is very over-bent. This fault is most likely to have resulted from a halt that was not enough in front of the rider's aids.

capable of stepping back. Most difficulties occur when the horse does not understand or, more likely, does not fully accept the rider's aids when going forward.

You can start preparing for this exercise very early on by asking the horse to step back in hand. It is easier for the horse to step back without the rider's weight on his back, because he has to bring his back up in order to move with clear and fluent (soft) steps. It is important to understand that when the horse is using himself correctly he steps back in a diagonal two-time rhythm and forward in a clear four-time rhythm. The rider should not ask a horse to rein-back when the aids are not fully accepted and there is insufficient connection between leg and hand.

The most common problem arises when the horse resists against the rider's hand and, because of this, pushes his head up and his back down, making it physically very difficult for himself to step back. Being forced to move back 'out of shape' makes a horse feel uncomfortable and leaves him with a bad experience in his mind, which will doom the next attempt.

There are quite a few versions of an incorrect rein-back: for example, too slow or rushing back (in both cases it will be difficult to control the number of steps); going off the bridle or becoming

A rein-back in training. The horse keeps a good outline and clearly lifts the right front leg and left hind leg off the ground at the same time. We can also detect a slight lowering of the hindquarters which ensures that the weight stays off the forehand.

crooked; or even resisting so strongly that the horse stays rooted to the spot. I think all these problems lead back to a horse's fear of the rein-back because he has had a bad experience with it and has been left with the impression that it is terribly difficult.

It is important that the rider finds a way of removing this fear and shows the horse that he can step back comfortably. In difficult cases you must take time and start in hand again. Once the horse is happy with that he can be asked to rein-back from the ground with a rider just sitting there, and as his confidence increases, the rider can slowly take over.

When asking for the rein-back the rider should transfer his weight slightly more onto his thighs to allow the horse to bring his back up. The hands can vibrate or give a few little half-halts; the legs should be on the horse's sides, but mainly to guide the straightness rather than to push. To stop the rein-back, the rider sits down on his seatbones again and the legs come on more strongly to increase the connection to the hands. This confirms that the horse is in front of the rider's forward aids and allows the rider to decide whether to halt or move forward.

The horse should stay at all times in front of the rider's legs, especially when stepping back. The halt obviously plays an important part in the rein-back. If the halt has been against the hand and unbalanced it will very easily continue through into the rein-back. If the halt has not been fully established, the rein-back will be anticipated and the horse will come behind the rider's forward aids. The halt and the rein-back must be assessed very much together.

Increasing submission

The degree of submission in a horse is related to how supple he is. You can pull a horse together if you are physically strong enough, and it might look as if you have him together enough to do most things, but it is not the right sort of submission. If it is forced too much, so that the horse is only responding out of a certain obedience, he will never have the flair that he could have if willingly submissive, when his individual personality is allowed to come through. However, a horse will want to be submissive only if his body is soft enough and gymnastic enough to respond to your aids. Submission does not stand on its own; it is preceded by relaxation, suppleness and acceptance of the aids.

Exercises like the permanently half-halting conversation, rein-back, shoulder-in, circles and transitions all help to maintain as well as improve submission. The submission takes place automatically because you are in fact working on it all the time, asking your horse to keep listening to you.

OPPOSITE PAGE: Ginny Leng and Master Craftsman taking a difficult line over a cross-country obstacle. This sort of accuracy is only possible if the horse is on the aids and in balance.

7

COMMON PROBLEMS

In all your work you have to bear in mind that the horse is always looking for an escape, an easy way out. Any hint of evasion requires early detection by the rider before it becomes a serious problem. The good rider who has a lot of feel can almost sense when the horse is just thinking about an evasion, and if he can nip the problem in the bud then it can easily be corrected. If you miss the early signs, and the evasion is allowed to develop, you may suddenly find that you have a major blockage on your hands. Checking the basic way of going and correcting any deficiencies on a daily basis will, in the long-term, keep a horse in good physical condition.

Stiffness

Nearly all horses are one-sided, but the problem is usually more obvious in young horses because it has not been dealt with. They have one side on which they feel better and more capable; the other side is slightly stiffer. You can detect this very early on, and by riding the horse forward from both legs into both reins you try to establish a neutral position, which is neither left nor right.

The reason why most horses are stiff on one side is because their body is naturally slightly curved to the other. You need to work more on the stiffer side to develop an independent, straight-through feeling, which will create the basis for equal bending.

Take the left rein, for example. Many people might describe their horse as being stiff on the left, or harder to the left hand, but in fact the horse is stiff on the right because he is not able to lengthen the muscles on the right side of his neck. This is because he is always going along in a slight curve (i.e. with the muscles shortened), so the muscles never get stretched enough.

It's quite common for the problem to change sides but every time it swaps, the stiffness is slightly less.

From the contact point of view, it's important to get the horse to accept equal weight on both reins so that you are able to establish the outside rein as easily to the right as to the left. Once you have bent the horse to one side, you can then loosen the inside rein, which makes the horse softer and teaches him to take care

The rider is attempting to perform a rein-back but the horse is resisting strongly against the rein, stiffening through the back and withers right down into the front legs. The rider looks sympathetic, and the resistance is most likely to be caused by a lack of suppleness in the horse's general way of going.

of himself from his inside hind leg.

If you do not establish the neutral position first, you will be forever pulling on the inside rein on his bad side, and you will not be able to let go because he is not taking the outside rein. If the inside rein is your only contact the horse will be heavy against that hand and block the inside hind leg coming through. If the inside hind leg cannot come through freely it will not support the weight and he will become heavier on the shoulder and therefore continue to lean even more against your inside hand. The whole thing can become a viscious circle.

Resistance

All resistances are based either on the wrong attitude or some physical discomfort (either caused by the exercise or because the horse is not feeling well). The rider must be open and sensitive to these things and respond to them. If you get any kind of resistance ask yourself what could be the cause. Sometimes a horse is just being awkward and needs a clear reminder.

Flatwork is done primarily to level out the horse's inefficiencies in his ability to use his body, so that he finds himself capable, both gymnastically and athletically, of doing the job you want him to do. Most resistances against movements, particularly lateral work and transitions, are based on the horse not being physically trained 'through'. The muscles are tight and won't give, and the horse naturally reacts to that by resisting any movement that his muscles cannot handle. Through your aids you have to

*This horse looks unhappy.
Judging by the strong hold that the rider has on the rein, the cause may be that the horse is not relaxed enough and does not want to be contained.*

make him use his body, often against his natural will, to help him become more gymnastic and develop the muscles he needs. For you to be able to do this the horse must have learnt to accept your aids, because only then will he be coerced into using his body slightly beyond what he would do by himself, and only then can you improve his athletic and gymnastic ability.

You can help your horse in his work by taking good care of his physical condition. You cannot expect him to stand in a stable for twenty-three hours and then come out and work to his best ability. He will need to have the chance, as you would yourself in a gymnastic class, to do a few preliminary exercises to loosen up the muscles. We know that when we do some stretching our muscles will ache initially, but that after a few exercises the muscles will give and feel more comfortable. Unfortunately the horse does not understand that. He feels his muscles aching, and physical discomfort is the main cause of resistance.

The rider needs to be encouraging but firm. You have to do the horse's thinking for him by taking greater charge and saying: 'Listen to me. I will help you through this.' This is where the horse's attitude comes in; he needs to be able to accept your help. If his attitude is negative and the horse is bossy and plays around whenever possible, he will use the discomfort as an excuse to object and try to get out of doing what you ask. A horse with the right attitude will try to accept the rider's aids over some discomfort, and the opportunity to do the exercise a few times will show the horse that he is physically able, and he will then have no cause to worry and will relax.

Once you start working a horse regularly you need to go through a three-phase work-out:

- Relaxing and suppling.

- Working.

- Relaxing and cooling off.

The last phase is really in preparation for the next time you ride. There are bound to be some exercises in which you have had to push the horse a little harder, so unless you make sure the muscles you have worked on are allowed to relax and cool off properly before they cut out (i.e. the horse stands still) the horse may well be stiff the next day.

Turning a horse out after you have ridden him is one of the best ways to relax and loosen his muscles, and it also relaxes a horse mentally. We spend a lot of time walking our horses. If they have been ridden in the morning they will often come out again in the afternoon for a walk.

When you first start to ride your horse you should work through a sort of check-list in your mind. The relaxation and suppling can take ten minutes, or more than half an hour – it depends on the horse and his age. Then you can take up a shorter contact, ask the horse to go forward between leg and hand, check his balance, his left and right bend, and basic transitions. If the horse feels stiff or is resisting in any of these basic exercises (even if he is a Grand Prix horse) you must stick with the basics until they are right. This is the best way to keep down the level of resistance.

Every problem, mental block, resistance or whatever starts off in a small way; a horse does not go from being perfect one moment suddenly to exhibiting some major resistance. The rider needs to be sensitive enough to notice when a problem first starts, because as long as it is small it does not take much to put it right. If it goes unnoticed (which often happens when a horse has a lot of ability and the rider goes straight into advanced movements, skipping some of the basics) then you eventually find that you have some serious problem with a particular movement. When this happens you have no choice but to go back to the root of the problem, a weakness in the basics.

Unsteady head carriage

If the head carriage is unsteady, this probably means that the bit has not been fully accepted and the horse moves on and off the bit, or tries to get away from one hand and then the other. There are many factors that can influence how well a horse accepts the bit. To start with, make sure that the horse is comfortable in his mouth – i.e. his teeth are in good order, there is nothing stuck in his gums (something as simple as a piece of oat stuck in the gum can cause an infection), and his tongue is not sore. Then, of course, the bridle must fit properly. Always eliminate all possible causes of discomfort before you insist on a horse accepting the bit, otherwise you are not being fair on him.

An unsteady head can also stem from an uncomfortable back. The horse may be naturally weak, or perhaps has pulled a muscle slightly, or has a badly fitting saddle. Sometimes a back problem can be difficult to spot. The horse may have twinged a back muscle in the stable without you realising, and if it isn't so bad that it makes him lame, you may not realise there is a problem. If, however, the unsteady head carriage persists after physical causes have been eliminated, the rider has to be firmer to make the horse accept the contact.

Head too high or too low

There are two extremes: the horse tries to lean on the hand or attempts to lift his head up and away from the contact. If either of these is happening you should consider how well the horse is accepting the bit by watching him on the lunge without a rider,

As you push a horse from behind to engage him more there are two main evasions that may occur. The first, illustrated here, is that the horse will lift up above the bit, which will make him hollow his back. This pushes the weight down through the withers onto the forehand.

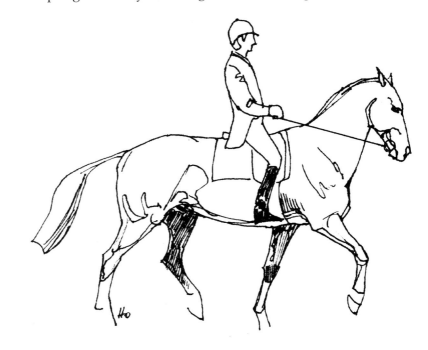

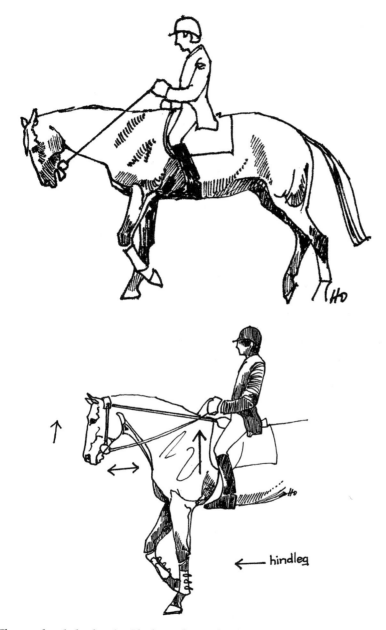

The second evasion is when the horse bears down on your hands, so that you push him onto the forehand. Further efforts to engage the horse can make the problem worse, and the head needs to be physically raised to bring it into a position whereby it will receive the engagement of the hind leg in the correct way.

← hindleg

The overhead check-rein. If a horse has to be constantly reminded to raise his head, the action may become too disturbing. If so, it may be necessary to use an overhead check-rein. This allows the rider's hands to remain still while ensuring that the horse has to take the increased engagement upwards into the rein. Once the horse understands the connection between leg and hand in this way, then consistent engagement will teach the horse to carry himself correctly.

The device shown in the picture has been adapted from a chambon head piece with plastic cord and simple clip attachments. When using the overhead check-rein the rider should ensure that the ordinary rein allows the horse to bring his nose forward, so that he is not restricted in his length of neck. Once a horse learns to carry himself correctly it will have a great impact on his presence.

to see how capable he is of carrying himself in a good steady outline. If the horse is having problems with his head carriage without a rider it is advisable to do some more work on the lunge.

If you have a horse that is bearing down so much that every time you try to push the hindquarters to achieve more engagement you just end up with weight going into your hand, you need to get the horse's head up before you start to push, so that any force from behind will then help to lift the horse up into the rein.

To do this you need to practise half-halts coupled with a little upward movement of one hand, to encourage the horse to raise his head. Don't keep nagging with the hands, because that won't really make the point. If after a few attempts you do not get the desired response then you need to try something else, otherwise you will be asking for the head to come up every 20 metres or so and this will be too disturbing for the horse.

The use of an overhead check-rein would help to stop the horse being physically able to put his head down, while the rider is able to push him from behind knowing that his head cannot disappear downwards. At the same time the rider can hold his reins quietly without having to chop the horse around.

This device needs to be used by an experienced rider. It should be introduced carefully, shortening the rein gradually. I have known horses change quite dramatically after using this rein. They usually have to be ridden in it only once or twice before they get the message that the push from behind means come up to the hand, and then they can be ridden with equal success without the device.

It is probably easier, for a less experienced rider, to deal with a horse whose head carriage is too high, because you can take the horse back to lungeing and work on the problem from there. You should find that if a horse has had a good base on the lunge and he has learnt to work, right from the beginning, with a low head carriage and has been allowed to stretch out forwards, he will quite quickly stretch down and forward onto the bit again.

If I have a horse who has been trained in the wrong way to the extent that the muscles have been built up too much underneath his neck, then I would also put him back on the lunge. If you try to ride him, he will set his muscles against you, and the more you ride him while he fights you, the more you will strengthen those muscles. Four to six weeks on the lunge with the horse going

The horse is working slightly behind the vertical but still engaging well, so the fault should be quite easy to correct, by the hand allowing the horse to step a little more out onto the rein.

Here the same horse is working slightly above the bit which results in hollowing and can be more damaging to the way of going than the previous fault.

correctly will weaken the lower neck muscles by not allowing him to use them. Then when you get on again you will find that the horse is no longer able to resist you in the same way, and you can start to build him up in the correct way.

On the forehand

To improve a horse that has a tendency to go on the forehand you need to confirm the contact and then work with half-halts and transitions, trying to increase the engagement. Once you have a good connection between inside leg and outside hand, you can start to use other exercises such as shoulder-in, but these exercises will not help unless you have achieved a reasonable level of carriage and engagement in the general trot and canter work.

Lack of engagement

A horse's physical attributes can affect his ability to engage his hind legs more effectively. A long back can be a disadvantage, but if the horse is able to angle his hind leg well through his joints he can make up for this. A horse with a short back and a stiff hind leg can have far greater difficulties.

If you have any problems with engagement you need to look at two things; is the back supple and is the horse accepting the contact? The back is the bridge between the front and back end of the horse, and if it is not supple and relaxed the hind legs cannot be affected enough by the forward aids. If the contact is not there, any energy created will be lost out the front onto the forehand. Everything is interconnected. You can improve a horse who, perhaps for some physical reason, finds it difficult to engage, by making sure all the basics are well accepted. If the back isn't free, then you will need to do some more suppling work and encourage the horse to stretch his head down. Once you have the contact and the horse is supple then you can start to work with transitions and half-halts, gradually getting the hind legs to come under more. This will automatically lighten the front and the horse will begin to carry himself better.

8

SOME THOUGHTS ON TACK AND EQUIPMENT

Saddles

I do not favour any particular make of saddle for dressage riding. What matters most to me is that it fits the individual horse well and that it is comfortable for him and, of course, comfortable for the rider. I have ridden in so many different saddles and I believe that if your seat is sound you can sit in any well-made saddle. There are certainly plenty of good saddles on the market these days.

The basic rules in fitting a saddle are that it should clear the horse's withers, and there should be no pressure points anywhere on the spine. The padding underneath the saddle should be even so that there is as much contact as possible with the horse's back, allowing the weight to be spread evenly over the area. The rider will want the saddle to be nicely balanced with a good, deep centre point; in other words not one that is up at the front and flat behind so that you feel as if you are sitting in an armchair, nor conversely (but less likely) one that tips the rider too far forward.

Bridles and bits

The stage at which you introduce the double bridle depends on how well a horse accepts the contact with the snaffle, and its use in competition is related to the level you have reached (it is is not permitted in dressage tests for novice event horses). If you think your horse is accepting the snaffle well, it doesn't hurt to try him in the double bridle quite early on so that you can find out more about the horse and how he will accept it. You shouldn't put a horse into a double bridle because you cannot ride him in a snaffle. On the other hand, you don't want to leave it to the last minute and try your horse in a double bridle only a few days before you do a test with one.

As long as your horse has learnt to accept the snaffle and work well on both reins there shouldn't be any problem in introducing

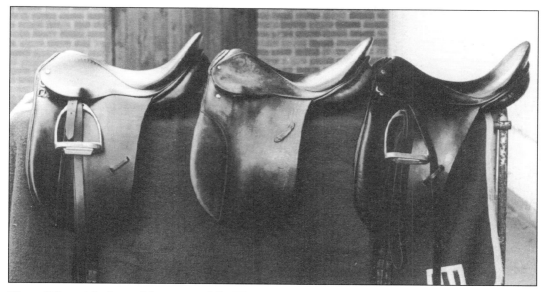

Three different designs of dressage saddle. The one in the middle is German made and the other two are British. The flaps on the first two saddles (left and centre) are similarly cut, both being fairly straight and of a good length. The third is cut slightly more forward, and the padding at the back of this saddle shapes away from the horse's back too abruptly so that it does not provide a consistent contact with the back. The padding should support the seat of the saddle right to the end.

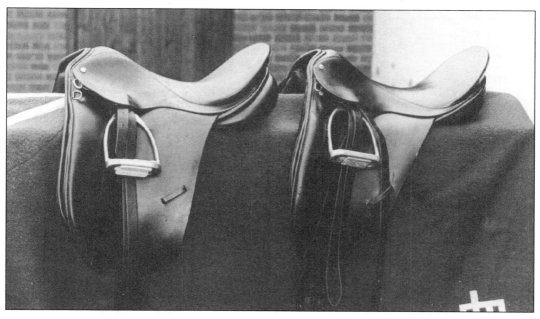

The deepest part of the seat should be close to the middle of the saddle. The saddle on the left is well balanced, but the one on the right has its deepest point too far back, which could easily put the rider in the wrong position.

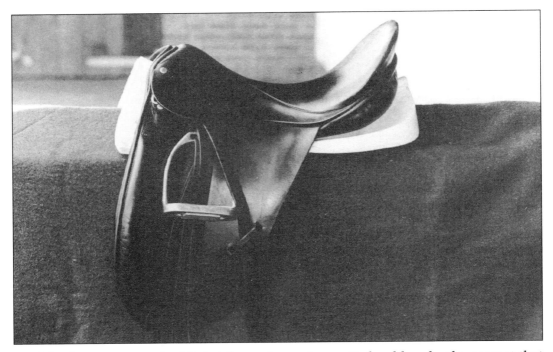

Special pads can help to make up for deficiencies in a saddle. The one shown here has an increased depth at the back, helping to move the deepest point of the saddle to the centre. This type of pad can also be useful on a horse with a high wither, as it compensates for the necessary height at the front of the saddle. Other pads can be used to soften or spread the contact over the back of the horse.

a double bridle, and once in use it should make the contact that little bit lighter and easier. If a horse goes quite happily in a double, I would normally do about two thirds of my work in a snaffle and a third in the double. However, you do find that some horses don't like the double bridle so much and they tend to back off it; if so, you have to ride them in it quite a lot. There may even be a period when you have to ride a horse consistently in a double bridle, until he fully accepts it, and then you can go back to doing some of your work in the snaffle.

The sort of bit you use for dressage will obviously depend on your horse, but remember to consult your rule book on the permitted types of snaffle, bridoon and curb bits. Bit guards, martingales and other gadgets (such as side-reins) are forbidden, as are any kind of boots and bandages. However, I always use boots and/or bandages for exercising at home.

Boots and bandages

I tend to put boots on the front legs and bandages behind because I feel that the boot will help to prevent a knock of some sort (which is more likely to happen on the front legs) whereas the bandages give more support to the hind legs, helping to prevent windgalls. This is particularly relevant in the pure dressage horse, where we put more and more emphasis onto the use of the hind legs.

These exercise boots are well padded with a double fastening. They offer good protection and are also comfortable.

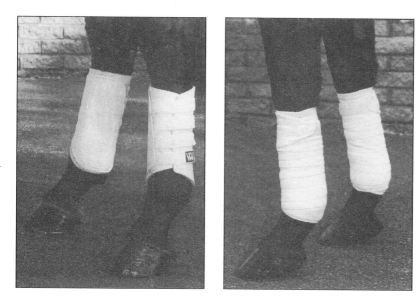

FAR LEFT: *A softer type of exercise boot which is very comfortable for the horse and is easy to use.*

LEFT: *Exercise bandages. These should be long enough (approximately 4 metres) and of good-quality material to offer both support and protection.*

The padding under these stable bandages is made of a material that allows the leg to breathe. It should be thick enough to help increase the horse's circulation and to protect the leg against any pressure points from the bandage. The bandage itself should be long and pliable, with a secure fastening.

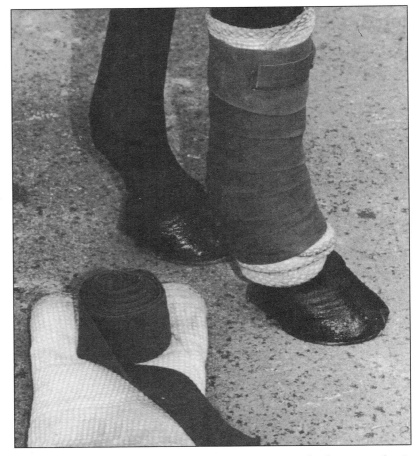

The bandages we use on our yard are very thick so we don't put any extra padding underneath them, and as long as they are reasonably new they usually have enough elasticity to prevent them being pulled too tight and damaging a horse's leg. However, putting them on does take a bit of practice and you need the right feel to know how tight to pull them. The best way to learn is to watch someone else do it, and then have a go yourself.

We also use bandages that are very long so that they can be closely overlapped on the way down the horse's leg, have plenty to spend to go around the fetlock for extra protection, and then come slowly up again. A long, thick bandage will both protect and support the horse's leg.

The horses on my yard in full training mostly wear stable bandages with padding underneath. These have two purposes: the first is protection, so that if a horse rolls in his stable and throws out a leg he is less likely to knock himself; the second is that they enhance the horse's circulation, which can prevent his legs from filling while he is resting.

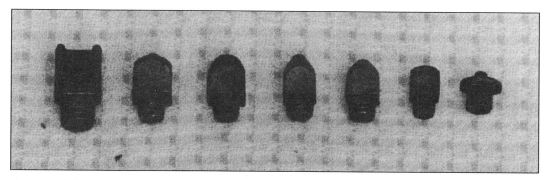

A range of the most common studs. I would normally use the ones in the middle of the range to help stay sure-footed in the dressage arena, and, unless the going was exceptionally bad, would put them in the hind shoes only. The stud on the right is a road stud.

Studs

Your horse may need studs for the dressage as well as for jumping. If you think the horse is likely to feel insecure because of the going you must do what you can to give him stability. However, unless the ground is very slippery, I don't like to use studs in the front shoes because they can have a stopping effect on the front action. This is particularly noticeable in the extensions because when the front foot hits the ground the stud stops it more abruptly. If your horse is off the forehand and reasonably well balanced, he shouldn't need much help from the front legs.

I would normally put studs in the hind shoes to make sure my horse didn't lose a hind leg going round a corner, for example. If a horse feels insecure about the going he will automatically stiffen a little, holding himself back and withdrawing his movement. This can have quite a dramatic effect on some horses.

Rider's equipment

Always consult your rule book at the beginning of the season to make sure there are no changes to the rules.

It is currently acceptable to wear a tweed riding jacket, shirt with collar and tie, breeches and plain black or brown boots for the dressage at a novice event. However, if you upgrade to intermediate you will need a black jacket, black boots and a white hunting tie (stock). You may wear a hunting cap (black or dark blue) or a skull cap with a black or dark blue cover. You won't need a top hat or tail coat until you reach advanced level or do an intermediate three-day event.

The correct dress for dressage at advanced and international level three-day events.

A rider correctly dressed for a novice or intermediate test at a one-day event. Spurs are optional at this level.

Whips are not permitted in the dressage arena (though you may use one when warming up) and spurs are optional at novice and intermediate level. Gloves must be worn at all levels.

9

COMPETITIONS

Riding-in at a competition

A competition atmosphere puts a heavy demand on a horse's concentration, and since his ability to cope with that atmosphere can only be worked on at a competition, you need to take your horse out to shows and events as soon as he is ready to go. Some horses are more vulnerable to the atmosphere than others, and you have to get to know your horse well so that you can predict how he will react to certain things. Then you can develop a specific system of riding-in to suit your horse.

There are two common problems associated with fit horses. One is that the horse comes out like a lion and wants to take on the world, but he will usually wind down and relax with the more work he does; and the other is that the horse tends to produce his best work during the first twenty minutes, but then becomes more and more excited, so that the more you work him the worse he becomes.

With the latter type it is no good just battling on in the hope that you will gradually wear them out, because by the time they are fit for eventing, particularly three-day eventing, they will have such a depth of stamina that you will find it difficult to drain their reserves. Even if you do eventually achieve a degree of co-operation, you will probably have taken the edge off your horse for the cross-country, and this could be critical at a three-day event when your horse needs to be feeling at his best for the speed and endurance day.

I have found that the best thing to do with the sort of horse who winds himself up is to take him out again and again, each time doing only a small amount of work before returning to the box. Every time you take him back to the box you need to untack him completely and perhaps even give him a small bite of hay so that he thinks he has finished for the day. Let him relax and settle down, and then an hour or so later take him out again. By about the second or third time the horse will start to think that he has done a lot of work, and in this way you begin to wear him down mentally rather than tire him physically. He will start to think, 'Not again,' and that will be the time his head drops a little and you can begin to put your legs on him and ask him to go forward. If you try to take him on while his mind is too keyed up,

A typical scene at a one-day event where horses have to be handled in and beside the horse-boxes. Having a well-mannered horse can make all the difference when trying to keep calm under competition pressure.

It can be useful to lunge your horse first to let him deal with any excess enthusiasm by himself.

you will find that he rebels and uses his strength against you, and then you will wear each other out. Half the amount of energy used in the right direction would be enough to achieve the same result.

You may have to take him out three or four times to achieve the desired result, but if you succeed with this method at a couple of events, the horse will learn to calm down and accept that there is nothing to be worried about. You will have shown him how to deal with his anxiety so that he can become more relaxed about the whole thing.

I always try to put the emphasis on achieving obedience through the mind as that is the best way to handle it in the long term, but a three-day event horse has to be so fit that calming the spirit sufficiently to obtain the obedience for the dressage test can be extremely difficult. You need to apply a lot of psychology!

The best way to help a very nervous horse is to keep your leg on him. At first he will probably reject your leg and try to run away from the contact and be over-active. But if you back off and take your leg away completely you will only increase the horse's insecurity and nervous state. You must ride the horse in a very positive but quiet manner and sit smoothly into his movement with your legs gently but consistently on his sides. If the horse has previously learnt to accept your leg he will find security, and your leg will gradually have a calming effect.

With the nervous or highly strung horse you need to be clear and consistent; don't pressurise the horse or get too strong, just hold out quietly for what you want. A lot of riders become inse-

There is usually plenty of space available for riding in, and you will soon get to know how much work your horse needs. Often horses are quite happy to work in around others but can change their behaviour quite drastically when asked to work alone in a dressage arena.

This horse is performing a movement that I couldn't find in any of the test sheets! However, the rider seems prepared to forgive.

cure in themselves when they feel that things are not working out; they begin to think that they must be doing something wrong and then change their tactics. But if you do that you may confuse the horse completely. Always try to give the horse the same sort of back-up and establish the basics in the same way. If you hold out for long enough you will usually achieve what you need.

You should not work in a confined space when a horse is so full of tension that he cannot settle. Forcing him into an outline and working in small circles will only serve to increase the tension, and the horse's attitude will be turned more and more against this type of work. Also, when a horse is too tense everything you try to do will feel extremely uncomfortable. If you insist on working him when his muscles are tight, he will operate in a cramped manner and, more importantly, could easily strain a muscle. Only relaxed muscles can respond successfully and be strong. Sometimes it is best to take the horse for a canter or even a gallop or even jump him a little so that he can let off steam, and then you can come back and try to make sense of the flatwork.

You want your horse to feel comfortable in his flatwork because then he will learn to enjoy it and automatically look upon it as a pleasant and relaxing alternative to all the hype of the cross country and show jumping, and his mind will approach it differently. If the horse sees flatwork as being something he is forced into and which makes him feel uncomfortable, then he is going to be against you before you even start.

Arena-craft

When you arrive at an event it is a good idea to have a quick look at the dressage arena in which you will ride to see what the going is like and make a mental note of any unevenness in the ground. If you are aware of any problems in advance you can give your horse that little bit more preparation in the test or, in muddy conditions, perhaps choose your line slightly differently to help maintain his rhythm.

Once you have done a few competitions you will have quite a good idea about how your horse responds to changes of environment and you will get to know when is the best time to take him into the collecting area for the dressage. You may need to vary your system to start with to find out what suits your horse best.

The main problem with event horses is persuading them to settle. The moment you enter the arena area after working in the collecting ring is when you feel the atmosphere most, even at a novice event. The horse also senses the atmosphere and, in addition, he suddenly becomes aware that he is on his own, which can have a dramatic effect on some horses. He might cope with the atmosphere quite happily as long as there are other horses or even people around him, but when you go to do your test he finds himself alone. This can be enough to trigger his excitement again, so it is best to keep him occupied; don't let his mind wander off and take in what is going on around him. Keep him busy.

In the time that you are given to ride around the arena before the hooter goes it pays to find out how much you can ask of your horse. At some competitions you will find the going in the arena is different to that in the collecting ring. You will need to get a feel for the new surface as you ride around the outside of the arena. I would be inclined to ask for a short piece of extension to find out how secure the going is and to assess how much I can ask from my horse, because the extended work in particular is dependent on how confident the horse feels on the going. He will need to adjust to the new surface and to the atmosphere, and he is bound to feel slightly different to the way he felt in the collecting ring. Some horses become lifted by the atmosphere and suddenly offer you a much better trot than they did outside, but others tense up and become more vulnerable to breaking their rhythm or breaking into canter.

Your horse may be expected to do his test when there are a lot of things going on around him. Your ability to hold his concentration will depend on how well he is prepared to listen to your aids.

Ian Stark and Murphy Himself proceeding accurately up the centre line.

If your horse starts spooking and playing up you can't really take him to task because you risk making him worse. At this stage it falls back on how well your horse has learnt to accept the aids at home. If this has been well established then you have a chance of overriding the outside influences and bringing the horse's attention back to you by coming on a bit stronger with the aids. But if you have always struggled to get him on the aids, even at home, then you have little chance of getting him to accept them there and then. In fact you are likely to upset things more by trying to force your aids on him, as he will use the outside influences as an excuse to resist you and you will end up losing control. Faced with a situation like that I would probably decide to try to smooth it over, and to keep the horse as calm as possible, but of course you cannot compete much on that basis. You need to have more true acceptance of the aids at home.

Remember, the horse will only be as relaxed as you are. Horses are quick to sense an occasion from you as well as the surroundings. If you can stay relaxed then you will be able to ride as well as you normally do, and this will help the horse. You obviously don't want to be so relaxed about the whole thing that you adopt the attitude that it really doesn't matter, otherwise you won't make the effort to get the best from your horse. You need enough adrenalin to want to do as well as you possibly can, but not so much that it blocks your feel and your capability as a rider.

Some people respond particularly well under pressure, as do some horses. The perfect combination is for both horse and rider to have a relaxed basis but to rise to the occasion under pressure, when it really matters. The best horses often have an inclination to show off, but without being worried. Horses who are taken over by nerves are much more difficult to contain and fragile to handle.

It can be helpful to talk through your test with another person as well as going through it in your mind, when you are not on a horse, so that you know the sequence of movements very well and the whole thing becomes second nature to you. When you enter the arena you know you have only one chance to do well and you are obviously under a certain amount of pressure. Everyone tends to tense up a bit, but the more familiar you are with the test the less you have to think about it, and the more you can concentrate on preparing and riding each movement.

Of course it is easy to make mistakes, especially if you are very nervous. If you do make an error of course you must quickly remind yourself that this mistake has nothing to do with the horse, it is purely down to you. You do not want to let the horse feel that you are dissatisfied with him, because then he may become tense. With any luck, as you hear the bell or hooter you

will instantly realise where you should have gone. If, however, you are completely lost, the judge will come out of his car or judge's box and tell you where you went wrong. Either way, you must go back to where the movement started and pick it up from there. In the heat of the moment it can be difficult to think clearly and do the right thing, but try to keep calm, keep your horse moving and quietly carry on as if nothing has happened.

At the 1990 Badminton horse trials when the new FEI test was introduced both Ian Stark and Ginny Leng made exactly the same error, one after the other. When Ginny made her mistake it was obvious from the buzz that went round the audience that she had gone wrong, but because she was so intent on what her horse was doing she did not notice the stir in the crowd and carried on until the bell went. It goes to show that riders go into a tremendously deep concentration when they are performing their dressage tests. If you can persuade your horse to concentrate equally well you have a good chance of getting the best from him.

Sometimes you will have to go into a test knowing that you have not yet gone far enough in your training to have fully established one or two of the movements required and that you are likely to have problems with these. However, you must not be so preoccupied with thinking about these problems that you let down the rest of your test. You should still ride everything as well as possible, and just accept some sort of compromise with

The correct execution of a movement depends largely on the degree of balance and preparation from the rider. Here we see the beginning of a 10m circle where the rider is looking ahead and the horse is well engaged and in self-carriage.

the movements that are not yet under the full control of your aids. You will find that you can often make up on the marks by concentrating on the things you can do really well, and if you can forget about any possible difficulties ahead the particular movement that was worrying you may well turn out far better than you expected.

You must keep your standards in the dressage arena and insist on the correct way of going, otherwise the horse may gain the impression that it doesn't matter what he does in the arena. You want the horse to learn to work in the arena with a 'business as usual' attitude. Only then can he become a reliable partner in competition.

You will obviously want to practise the movements for your test at home, but don't practise them in exactly the same sequence as the actual test because some horses quickly pick this up and start to anticipate the movements. The main thing is to practise the movements in an arena so that you and your horse become accustomed to working within its four corners and you learn to balance the horse in a more confined space. The horse will have to be more on your aids to improve his balance and to give you more control.

Riding in balance is the essence of arena-craft. If you can ride through the corners, straight down the centre line, and across the diagonal in balance it makes the horse look capable and confident. When faced with difficult going – slippery or uneven ground – you will be one step ahead of your fellow competitors if your horse is better balanced and you are able to help him by bringing him more under your seat and lightening the forehand. The ability to take the horse off the forehand gives you much greater control on a slippery surface and it allows the horse to put his feet down more securely and confidently.

Corners, in particular, are a reflection of how well a horse is in balance, how well he contains the engagement from behind and so on. In the dressage arena there is a corner coming up all the time, and if you can ride these well you have a good chance of doing the next movement well. Provided you can ride the corners in balance you can use them to your advantage. If, for example, you have lost a little engagement on a difficult movement, then you can regain it by using the next corner to remind the horse to come back on his quarters, so that you have a fresh start for the subsequent movement. If you cannot use the corners properly you will find that any problem in the previous movement will snowball, getting worse and worse, and you may not be able to regain your composure for the rest of the test. The corners are the key factor in a test. Get them right, and you have a much better chance of retaining or regaining the correct way of going.

As far as the different movements are concerned, fifty per cent of the execution lies in the preparation, so you must give your horse every possible chance by thinking ahead. This will also help your accuracy, which is of great importance, because you really do need to be spot on. There is a saying that nearly good is nothing else but bad. The same applies to your accuracy in a dressage test – you are either on the line or off it, and being near-ly on it is not good enough.

You need to develop a feel for the size of the dressage arena. A knowledge of the markers, and the distances between them, will enable you to work out exactly where you should be if, say, you are performing a 10-metre circle. If you have to change pace or direction at a particular place, this should happen as your knee comes level with the marker.

The markers and lines are clearly defined, and in your training towards a competition you should have made it very clear to your horse that it really matters to you that he stops here or turns on that particular line. It is very easy to fudge the accuracy. For example, on the short side of the arena many riders go from cor-ner to corner as if they were making a circle when instead they should ride the two corners individually with a straight line in between, just as they would do on the long side.

Karen Lende (USA) and Nos Ecus competing at Burghley in 1991. The big crowds at major competitions can give the atmosphere tremendous electricity, which makes it difficult for the ultra-fit horse to stay sufficiently relaxed.

I think it is important to regard test riding as part of a horse's training in which your objective is to establish in the horse the right attitude towards his work at a competition. It is no good being able to perform well at home but not at an event, where it counts. You want to be confident that you can work together with your horse at a competition just as well as you can at home, as this is the only way to ensure consistency and long-term success.

Judging

Once you put yourself and your horse in front of a judge you are being tested on how well the training has been established at a given level and how consistently your horse performs. At the same time a test should give the rider a guide to how, and with what priorities, he should be working with his horse in the future.

There are two major points in assessing how well or badly the test is performed: the first is the general way of going; the second is the correct execution of the individual movements. The tests are structured so that the horse can be assessed from the moment he enters the arena to the moment he leaves it. That means that the horse's way of going at a corner, or along the short side of the arena, belongs either to the last movement or the start of the next one, and will be included in the mark. This puts a very high demand on the consistent balance of the horse and on the rider to lead and position his horse correctly through the figures required. Many marks can be gained or lost through this. The rider is responsible, through having the horse on his aids, for the horse's balance, thus helping him to maintain a good rhythm and natural paces through all the different movements.

The purpose of the dressage test, apart from the competitive aspect, is to obtain confirmation or help in the further training of the horse, but unfortunately in both pure dressage and event dressage there are not enough useful comments given on the test sheets to assist in a horse's training. Often a mark of five or six will be given without any comment, yet in the early stages of competition it is really the comment that is more valuable than the mark. Obviously the mark will affect your placing, but if the judge could point out why a particular movement was not performed satisfactorily, this would be far more beneficial for the training.

In Chapter 11 I have gone through three dressage tests, at novice, intermediate and advanced (FEI) level, talking about the movements required, how they should be performed, how they should be judged, and what they will do for the training of the

horse. I hope that these analyses of the different tests will give further guidance in the preparation of a horse for competition.

The end of the season

A novice horse is still in the process of building up his strength and muscles, and has probably not yet gained a good, solid foundation in his flatwork, so if you allow him a complete break, say six weeks or more out in the field, at the end of the season, his basic work is likely to deteriorate. It is a good idea, therefore, to let the horse down from eventing fitness but to keep up the flatwork. Because he is less fit, he should be calmer, and this will allow you to make more progress on his flatwork and at the same time keep him occupied so that he doesn't get bored. Now is the time to further his education.

Once a horse has become more established and done a good season's work then he probably needs a complete break. He should be let down slowly by easing off his work for a week or two after a competition. In my opinion, turning him straight out to grass the day after an event is too drastic for the system. Hard food and work should be slowly faded out.

Quite often a horse that is well established in his training can benefit significantly from a complete break. He may, for example, have had difficulty in learning something and become tense about it, creating a sort of mental block; perhaps either the rider or the horse had been trying too hard and had become tight.

Between one and three judges assess a class, depending on the level of competition. They are positioned on the short side at the C end of the arena. Each judge will have a slightly different view of the movements performed, which can result in minor discrepancies in the marks. However, there should never be serious differences in opinion when assessing a movement.

When the horse comes back into work again you sometimes find that a movement he had previously found difficult comes more easily to him, because the break has helped the training to sink in and has taken away the tension. Once a horse has learnt the aids and understands the movements properly he will never forget them.

Ginny Leng's Priceless (1986 World Champion) and Ian Stark's Glenburnie (1991 European Champion) are good examples of well-established horses who, through illness or injury, had to be laid off for a year, and who came back after their break better than ever.

10

MORE ADVANCED TRAINING

The right training, on a daily basis, will help to improve the deficiencies in your horse and raise the quality of his work to a higher level. All the time your horse will be developing and becoming stronger, so that you can gradually introduce different movements. However, it is no good trying to work to a strict schedule of progress; you have to just do as much as you feel your horse is capable of and take each day as it comes.

There will be days when your horse comes out of his box feeling as if he could take on the world. Everything seems to go right, and you think, 'Gosh, this is easy.' But then the next day, when you are planning to go on from there, you find you are back to square one. The good days, when you can mentally tick off all the basics very easily, are the days when you can make a move to progress to a more advanced movement – perhaps a shoulder-in or a half-pass. The following day the horse may be less supple or not bending properly. When that happens you must re-establish the basic links, rather than trying a more advanced movement without the right basis. You can't say, 'Well, yesterday we did the shoulder-in, so today we must move on to the next thing.' It doesn't work like that.

When you have had a day when the horse has felt terrific and you were able to ask for more, the horse often stretches muscles and ligaments that he may not have used as much before, so the next day he comes out feeling a little stiff and achy. The rider needs to be aware of how his horse is feeling, and how much he can expect to ask of him. Some days you have to be prepared to work for the basics and leave it at that.

Medium and extended paces

Assuming the horse is working well between leg and hand, i.e. he is going freely forward and accepting the contact, the rider can start working to improve the engagement of the hindquarters, and with it the balance necessary to develop medium paces. If the horse is not accepting an equal contact and the half-halt

Richard Meade with Kilcashel at the World Championships in Luhmühlen in 1982. He is performing the medium trot on a circle from the old FEI test. The horse is swinging nicely through in good self-carriage, and the rider is clearly concentrating on keeping the horse balanced on the curve.

Ian Stark and Murphy Himself at Badminton in 1989. They are doing the extended trot across the diagonal and the horse is pushing powerfully from behind, getting a good length of stride with a good neck and head carriage. Ideally the horse could have achieved a little more lift in the shoulder.

correctly, the rider will find it difficult to the keep the weight off the forehand as he asks for more impulsion. A good medium pace will only be possible if the horse is supple over his back and capable of carrying, as well as pushing, with the hind legs.

Improving the balance, which means increasing the engagement of the hindquarters and the lightness of the forehand through the use of transitions and half-halts, will make the horse able and more confident to hold a clearer rhythm and a bigger stride. All kinds of transitions are helpful, but in particular transitions within the trot will help to develop the collection needed to produce better medium or extended paces.

Although a degree of collection will be needed before the horse can be expected to extend, there must be a full commitment from the horse to want to go forward. Some horses lack confidence and won't let go of themselves, so you have to ride forward for some time until the horse finds out that he can, through relaxing and swinging in his back, achieve a bigger rhythm.

As the horse's confidence grows, the rider can go back to working in a more collected way and then let the bigger stride come as a relief from the increased flexion of the hock. In this way the desire to go forward will be increased and, as the horse offers to go more forward by himself, the rider will find it easier to look after his balance and the horse will learn to hold a rhythmical extension in balance for longer distances. Every time the rider feels the horse's balance going too much onto the forehand it is better to bring it back using repeated half-halts and to point out the loss of self-carriage by asking the hind legs to step under the body again and carry more weight. As the horse becomes stronger and more confident he will be able to reach his full forward-moving capacity.

Collection

As described earlier, collection is the ability of the horse to lower and engage the hindquarters, which helps him to become lighter on the forehand. The moment a horse is capable of carrying more weight on his hind legs he will achieve a much better balance, which is why it is useful to work towards collection even though it is not required in event tests. Collection is a gradual process because it relies on the physical development of the horse. The conformation and the gymnastic ability of the individual horse is, of course, very relevant to how well and how quickly a horse will learn to collect.

Because collection is achieved progressively, there are varying levels of it, and different movements require different degrees of collection. If the horse is capable of performing a movement like a 5-metre circle of the correct size and shape with consistent rhythm and fluency, and with self-carriage, then he has achieved true collection.

The rider can use collection to improve the balance, submission and expression of the stride. There is quite a difference in the quality of trot between a horse who is capable only of a working trot and one who is capable of a collected trot but ridden forward to a working trot. There is no reason why the advanced event horse shouldn't be trained beyond the standard of the FEI test.

The piaffe is the ultimate degree of collection and is asked for only in Grand Prix and Grand Prix Special dressage tests. The quarters lower to take on most of the weight, allowing the shoulder to lighten and the motion to stay on the spot. The author on Giovanni, working in before their test at Aachen.

As well as improving the horse's paces and way of going it will help to make him more athletic in his body and keep the work on the flat interesting.

Counter-canter

The natural crookedness of a horse is most noticeable in the canter. On one rein the horse likes to put his quarters to the inside more than on the other, therefore it is important that he learns to centralise his balance and become straight. It is necessary for the horse to be well established in the acceptance of the aid to canter on both reins before counter-canter is attempted.

The transition into canter should be possible from trot and from walk. The two main requirements needed to perform the counter-canter are a balanced bend and impulsion. As with all other movements, it is important that the horse is well prepared before you try the movement for the first time. It is up to the rider to show the

Counter-canter performed in training. The horse is staying nicely bent to the leading leg of the canter, and both horse and rider look well balanced and straight.

horse what is required to execute a movement well and easily.

Riding a little shoulder-forward in the canter is a good exercise to improve straightness and confirm balance through increased inside leg and outside rein contact. Smaller circles help the rider to assess and improve the degree of impulsion/engagement and balance in the canter before he attempts the counter-canter. Also, riding shallow loops on the long side and returning to the track after a half circle will help to introduce and prepare the horse for what is to come. The better the impulsion and balance in the basic canter, the easier it will be for the horse to get round a turn in counter-canter.

It is much more difficult to perform the counter-canter in an arena, or any enclosed space, than it is in an open field, because the horse naturally backs off the surroundings and loses balance to the inside. This often results in one of the most common mistakes seen in dressage tests: the rider tries to hold onto the canter by pulling the horse's head to the outside, but this forces the shoulder to fall to the inside and, as a result, the hindquarters are thrown out. The hind legs are then unable to support the main weight of the horse and he finds it very difficult to maintain a fluent canter. In severe cases, this loss of balance makes the horse

This diagram shows counter-canter on the straight and on a bend. The rider holds the horse balanced between inside leg and outside rein – the inside leg keeping the inside hind leg of the horse engaged while the outside leg contains the quarters. The inside rein stays soft and renews the bend.

lose the canter or change the lead in front to compensate.

It is important to understand that the inside of the horse is now with the lead of the canter and is facing the outside of the arena. The horse stays clearly positioned with the lead of the canter, and should remain on the rider's inside leg and outside rein contact – this will help to keep the horse's inside hind leg more under the weight and the balance in the centre. In this way the horse will be able, with a little practice, to maintain a good counter-canter.

Lateral work

To start lateral work you must have full co-operation from your horse. If the aids are fully accepted and the horse is supple in his work to the left and to the right there should be no major problem.

The rider must assess the quality of the work building up to lateral exercises and deal with any deficiencies and any problems in the basic work. For example, problems such as unlevel contact, the horse not in front of the leg, tight in the back or lacking bend, will become worse when you start lateral work, allowing the horse to withdraw or escape further from the aids.

Shoulder-in

Working towards riding a correct shoulder-in will help the rider improve his horse's engagement, flexion and balance. Perfecting this movement relies mainly on the horse accepting the rider's inside leg and outside rein. The rider's inside leg (positioned on the girth) asks for increased engagement of the inside hind leg while the consistent contact with the outside rein leads the shoulder-in. The inside rein looks after the flexion of the neck to the inside, while the rider's outside leg (positioned behind the girth) has a more passive, holding function and is there to keep the quarters based on the line. The rider's weight is slightly more on the inside seatbone.

For the angle required in test riding you have to bring the horse onto three tracks so that the inside hind leg follows the line of the outside foreleg. For training purposes it is sometimes necessary to vary the degree of angle to work against any natural (undesired) tendency offered by the horse. For example, horses will often try to avoid bending on their stiff side by offering too much angle, while on the other side they may offer too much bend in order to avoid the angle. It is, therefore, very important that the rider is aware of this and can vary the angle used in training in order to ensure that the horse learns to use itself

The ideal angle and bend for the shoulder-in as it is performed in a test. The diagram shows the three tracks and the main aids of the rider.

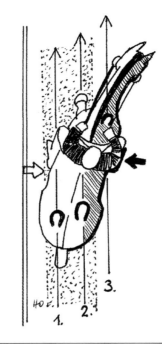

There are many ways of doing a shoulder-in and the possibilities for evasions are great. This horse is showing hardly any angle and is trying to absorb the rider's aids through the bend by tipping in from the poll. To correct this the rider needs to confirm equal contact on both reins and increase the connection between inside leg and outside rein to create more angle.

This horse is showing the wrong bend for a shoulder-in left, which almost converts it into a renvers. The fault should be fairly easy to put right if the rider gives the correct aids and asks for a clear left bend.

A good working shoulder-in with the angle slightly increased to put a little more demand on the engagement and the crossing over of the inside hind leg. The horse shows exceptionally nice bend and carriage.

equally on both reins.

Sometimes the correct amount of angle needs to be seen in relation to the individual horse. When on three tracks, a narrow-striding horse will appear to be showing far less angle than a wider-striding horse.

It is helpful to develop the shoulder-in from a small circle or out of a corner because there has already been demand a for increased engagement of the inside hind and inside flexion. Very often the horse will back off in order to avoid the rider's request for increased engagement, which is required by the degree of angle; in this case, the rider should be satisfied with less angle to start with, and concentrate on increasing the forward flow. On that basis the angle can be increased again more successfully.

The shoulder-in continues to be an invaluable exercise throughout the horse's training since it can be used for loosening purposes as well as in preparation for more difficult movements.

Travers and renvers

These exercises are very useful for working on the horse's ability to bend around the inside leg. They are performed along a

Here we see a good travers to the right. The horse is looking well engaged, and his expression suggests that the trot is fluent.

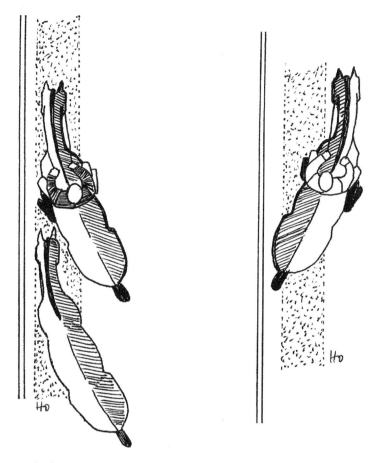

FAR LEFT: *The travers right. The horse is flexed in neck and body; the rider's inside leg is still responsible for the engagement, while the outside leg pushes the horse around the inside leg to create the angle. The weight is slightly more on the inside seatbone, and the outside rein holds a more constant contact while the inside rein creates the bend and stays light.*

LEFT: *Renvers. This is basically a mirror-image of the travers and the same aids apply.*

straight line, so the rider does not have to worry about directing the horse across the arena.

In travers the horse is bent to the inside of the neck and is also bent around the rider's inside leg in the body; he brings his quarters in to the arena with more angle than in the shoulder-in. The trot should stay engaged and fluent, so it is important to keep a forward-flowing trot while slowly increasing the amount of angle. If the horse finds it difficult to maintain fluency while being asked to cross over for a half-pass, then the travers can help to give him confidence and assist him in finding his balance.

The renvers is the same principle as the travers, but it is positioned against the wall of the arena instead of away from it, which makes it slightly more difficult and the horse has to listen more carefully to the rider's aids. I find the renvers useful for encouraging independent bend and balance in a horse.

If your horse is supple and gymnastic it should be possible to interchange the different lateral movements and angles fluently from one to another, without changing rhythm and outline.

Half-pass

Like all lateral work the half-pass is based on a good connection between hand and leg and the correct positioning of the horse into the desired direction. The basis of a good half-pass is a correct shoulder-in, so this must have been well established on both reins before any attempt is made at the half-pass.

Many riders think that in half-pass the horse should go sideways, so they push the quarters over with their outside leg, and thus make it very difficult for the horse to maintain a rhythmical and fluent trot. It is important to keep the horse thinking forward when the rider starts working in half-pass.

Most problems in half-pass are due to insufficient acceptance of a contact from leg to hand and lack of bend in the neck and ribs. The bend in the neck should be independent from the bend in the body. The rider must really understand why and how all the aids are working together. Is the horse working well in front of the rider's leg into both reins? Is he supple and engaged? The rider must then ask for an inside bend and take a clearer connection between inside leg and outside rein. This brings the horse close to a shoulder-in position.

A half-pass to the right. The horse is pulling diagonally forwards and sidewards with a good, clear bend. The rider is keeping beautifully in balance with the horse.

It should now be possible to start a half-pass or, in cases where the bend is more difficult, it may be better to prepare with one or more smaller circles. When you go into the half-pass you lead the horse from your outside rein into the new direction and keep him bending round your inside leg. The inside rein creates the bend and then lightens, and is there to renew the bend if necessary.

The outside leg (behind the girth) asks the horse to bend round the inside leg and to move sideways, while the inside leg looks after the forward movement. The rider's weight is more on the inside seatbone to encourage the horse to step in this direction. The inside leg plays an important role, as not only is the bend held around it, but also it looks after the engagement and cadence of the horse's inside hind leg.

A half-pass should be assessed from three aspects:

- The quality and reach of the trot step.

- The correct and clear bend in neck and body.

- The balance and fluency with which the horse stays parallel from marker to marker.

The left halt-pass. Again the horse is nicely bent in the neck. The head and neck lead the direction of travel, followed by the shoulder and then the quarters. The quarters should step up to be parallel with the shoulder, through the bend in the body. The rider is straight above the horse, but could sit a fraction more on the inside (left) seatbone.

The horse should be parallel with the long side, with the head and neck leading in the direction of the half-pass. If the horse is not parallel he will be either trailing or leading with his quarters.

Problems with the bend occur when the horse is not correctly on the outside rein or is generally one-sided. He will either lift his head and bend only from the nose, or he will tip into the bend from the poll and come behind the vertical. In this case, the rider must establish a better contact into both reins and improve the connection between inside leg and outside rein.

A good, consistent contact, mostly on the outside rein, and the acceptance of a forward-pushing inside leg, are of the utmost importance because the fluency and rhythm of the trot depend on them. The rider should always keep in mind that the half-pass is a forward/sideways movement and that, although it appears to be parallel with the long side the horse must be asked and allowed to pull diagonally down the line of the half-pass to ensure a rhythmical and fluent trot.

Once all the different lateral movements are established they need to be checked and practised regularly as they play an important part in the daily gymnastic work of the horse. With a more advanced horse, the lateral work can also be used in the 'loosening-up' phase, particularly with naturally stiffer horses.

A common fault in the half-pass: the quarters are leading and the poll is tipping back in the bend. It is very difficult for a horse in this position to maintain a free-flowing trot. This horse is not enough between the inside leg and outside rein, and to correct the fault the rider would have to return to a good shoulder-in and then start the half-pass again from that basis.

In this half-pass to the right the horse is showing quite a nice bend, although the rider has lost contact with her inside leg. This could result in the horse losing cadence and balance. The rider has a good contact on the outside rein, but has locked her left elbow.

The interesting thing is that the lateral ability of a horse never stays exactly the same. Most horses have a basic preference to one side but this can often change around and the rider has to be very sensitive to any variation. Early detection to avoid deterioration is the answer and, above all, attention to the basic way of going, as any lateral movement can only be as good as the basic gait in which it is performed.

11

THREE TESTS ANALYSED

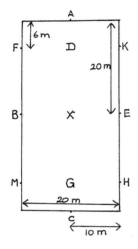

20m x 40m arena.

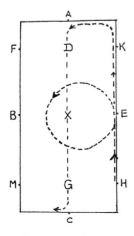

Movement 2.

Horse Trials Dressage Test C (Novice Standard) 1987

Arena 20m x 40m.
To be ridden in a snaffle.

MOVEMENT 1

A	Enter at working trot.
X	Halt. Salute. Proceed at working trot.
C	Track left.

The horse should be straight and balanced down the centre line, the working trot of good quality. The transition into the halt and back to the working trot should be clear and smooth without any resistance against the hand or leg. In the halt the horse should stand attentive and well balanced on all four legs. From the judging point of view, a straight well-balanced transition with a less than perfectly square halt should be marked higher than a square halt with a resistant transition, because it will make the priorities clear to the rider in his training of the horse. This being the first impression the judge will get from the horse and rider, it is a very important movement.

MOVEMENT 2

E	Circle left 15m diameter.
A	Down centre line.
C	Track right.

The circle should be the correct size and the horse should be bent to the circle line. The judge will look for impulsion and consistent rhythm of the trot, and will try to assess the balance and bend to both sides when turning onto and off the centre line. The horse should be completely straight when on the centre line.

MOVEMENT 3

B   Circle right 15m diameter.
FAK   Working trot.

The same applies as on the left. Particularly interesting to the judge will be the difference in bend and balance from the left to the right side.

MOVEMENT 4

KXM   Change rein and show some lengthened strides.
M   Working trot.

The horse should use his natural ability and cover more ground with increased impulsion and regular strides. Because he is asked for only *some* lengthened strides, the transitions can be progressive. The judge likes to see some lift from the shoulder through the increased impulsion from behind.

MOVEMENT 5

C   Halt – Immobility 4 seconds.
           Proceed at medium walk.

The transition in and out should be smooth and show no resistance. The halt must be well placed at the marker – ideally with the rider's knee at C. In the halt the horse should be square and support his weight on all four legs. The horse should remain at halt for 4 seconds, on the rider's aids and in a good and steady outline.

MOVEMENT 6

HXF   Change rein at free walk on a long rein.
F   Medium walk.
between
F&A   Working trot.

The horse should stretch himself well forward and, with a good four-time rhythm, cover as much ground as possible. It is important that while on a long rein the horse retains a purposeful and marching stride well onto the line of the diagonal. There should be no resistance or unsteadiness when picking up the rein for the transition to medium walk and working trot.

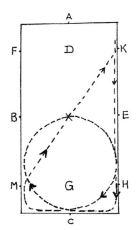

Movement 7.

MOVEMENT 7

between
A&K	Working canter right.
C	Circle right 20m diameter.
MXK	Change the rein.
K	Working trot.

There is a lot to assess with one mark. The transition into canter should be clear, balanced and with no change of the outline. The judge will assess the rhythm, impulsion and straightness of the working canter, which continues onto a 20-metre circle at C. Here the consistency of the canter and the correct size and bend of the circle are important. There is an extra demand on the accuracy of the rider and the control he has over his horse's balance. When the horse is on the track of the whole arena he should go into the corners, but when on a circle he should follow the circle line and stay out of the corners. It is important that a clear difference is shown; this will be particularly clear in this movement, because we have two corners in succession which have to be ridden differently. The canter continues onto the diagonal, where again balance and straightness are required. The transition back to working trot should be on the marker and stay off the forehand. A clear trot rhythm should be established from the first step and there must be left bend through the corner.

MOVEMENT 8

between
A&F	Working canter left.
C	Circle left 20m diameter.
HXF	Change the rein.
F	Working trot.

This mirrors the sequence above, but on the left rein. The well-trained horse should be able to show rhythm, balance and fluency equally on both sides.

MOVEMENT 9

A	Down the centre line.
G	Halt. Salute.
	Leave arena at walk on a long rein at A.

There should be a balanced turn down the centre line. Straightness and consistent impulsion should be held down to G, and a straight and square halt established.

Collective marks

10. General impressions, obedience and calmness.
11. Paces (freedom and regularity) and impulsion.
12. Position and seat of the rider and correct use of the aids.

The collective marks should reflect the general impression of the whole test, and the judges have the chance to underline their opinion of the horse's way of going and the rider's position, but it is the comments behind the marks which are most helpful for the rider.

NB: In BHS and Horse Trials Novice Tests, trot work may be executed either 'sitting' or 'rising' at the discretion of the rider.

Competing at the Seoul Olympics: J. Michael Plumb (USA) and Adonis.

Horse Trials Dressage Test K (Intermediate Standard) 1984

Arena 20m x 40m.
To be ridden in a snaffle or simple double bridle.

MOVEMENT 1

A   Enter at working trot.
X   Halt. Salute. Proceed at working trot.

This movement has the same demands as in the novice test, although the judge will expect a higher standard and better balance in the horse's way of going.

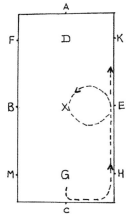

Movement 2.

MOVEMENT 2

C   Track left.
E   Circle left, 10m diameter.

Having to ride the smaller circle will test if the horse has learnt to bend and engage more. The judge is again looking for consistency in size, bend and rhythm.

MOVEMENT 3

A   Down the centre line.
C   Track right.

The combination of left turn, straight line, right turn is a good movement to tell the judge about the accuracy of the rider and the balance of the horse. The horse should bend equally well turning onto and off the centre line, and be completely straight and fluent on it.

MOVEMENT 4

B   Circle right, 10m diameter.

The same circle is now asked for on the other rein, and it is interesting for the judge to see how far the horse is in his training of becoming equal on both sides.

MOVEMENT 5

A   Halt. Rein-back 4 steps. Proceed at medium walk

The halt at A should be accurate, balanced and square. The rein-back is quite a test of submission and suppleness of the horse. Although the judge has to look for the right number of steps, the correctness and quality should count more. There must be a fluent transition into medium walk.

MOVEMENT 6

KXM   Change rein at free walk on a long rein.
M   Medium walk.

The free walk on a long rein shows the natural ability of the horse to lengthen his frame and cover the ground. Apart from looking for a good rhythm and size of step, the judge will assess how obedient and consistent the horse stays through the transitions from medium walk and back again.

MOVEMENT 7

C   Working canter left (directly from walk).

This very testing transition is marked on its own to show the importance of the movement at this standard. The preparation goes back to the last movement when the horse comes back to medium walk and has to accept all the rider's aids again after having been on a long rein. The canter transition should be clear and fluent. The judge should prefer a horse who does a fluent but slightly progressive transition, and remains on the aids, to one who goes immediately into canter, but is abrupt and comes off the rider's aids at that moment.

MOVEMENT 8

E   Circle left, 15m diameter.

The circle should be nice and round, and the correct size. The consistency of bend and flow depends a lot on how well the horse is engaged, and stays engaged, on the circle.

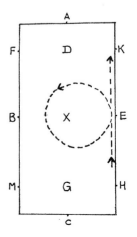

Movement 8.

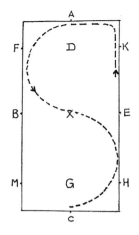

Movements 9 and 10.

A   Half circle left, 20m diameter to X.

The half circle starts at A, so it is important to go into the corner before A and to arc round the next corner to the required line of the circle. It is of great importance to prepare the canter for the oncoming transition at X. In fact, movements 9 and 10 are very closely linked together and influence each other's mark.

X   Simple change of leg, and half circle right 20m diameter to C.

The simple change of leg is, apart from the medium paces and 10m circles, the biggest criterion at this standard. There are two difficult transitions very close together. There should be a clear transition into walk, followed by two or three correct walk steps and a clear transition into canter again. The mark will depend mostly on the correct place (over X), the clear transitions (canter, walk, canter) and the fluency of it all.

B   Circle right, 15m diameter.

The same applies as in Movement 8.

A   Working trot.
KXM   Change rein at medium trot.
M   Working trot.

The transition to trot should be smooth and on the mark. The horse should find a clear rhythm and self-carriage from the first step. For the medium trot on the diagonal the horse must show good engagement and cover the ground as well as gaining more height. The transitions into medium and back to working trot are assessed within the same mark and should be fluent without any disturbance in the rhythm.

HXF   Change rein at medium trot.
F   Working trot.

The same applies as in Movement 12. It usually helps the horse to be able to do a second medium trot straight after the first one, and one often finds that the second one is better.

MOVEMENT 14

A   Down centre line.
G   Halt. Salute.
             Leave arena at walk on a long rein at A.

The last centre line is a real test of obedience again, because some event horses sense the end of the test coming and become strong as they approach G. The horse who can contain himself, stay straight and produce a square halt will earn a good mark. Also, this last impression can have either a positive or negative influence on the collective marks.

Collective marks
1. Paces (freedom and regularity).
2. Impulsion (desire to move forward, elasticity of the steps, suppleness of the back and engagement of the hindquarters).
3. Submission (attention and confidence: harmony, lightness and ease of the movements; acceptance of the bridle and lightness of the forehand).
4. Position, seat of the rider, correct use of the aids.

There are four collective marks given in all the higher-level tests. The real addition is the mark for submission, which reflects the way in which the horse has carried out the more difficult movements and transitions.

NB: In BHS Elementary or Horse Trials Intermediate Tests all trot work is executed 'sitting'.

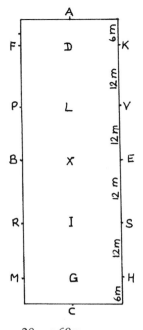

20m x 60m
arena.

The FEI Three-day Event Dresssage Test (Senior) 1990

Arena 20m x 60m.

This new FEI test was developed and tried in 1989 and has now replaced the old one. The new test breaks up the old patterns well and most significantly has got rid of the very difficult medium trot circles and includes shoulder-in on the long sides. There is twice a sequence of medium/extended walk which breaks up the canter movements and is very good to test how well the horse is on the aids. This is the only event test where this is included.

MOVEMENT 1

A	Enter at working canter.
I	Halt. Immobility. Salute.
	Proceed at working trot.

The entry should be nice and straight with a square and settled halt at I. Having to halt beyond X will catch out the horses who think they know the test and the rider has to ride the canter very positively to the marker. As in all tests, the rider can choose which lead in canter he uses to enter on, and the thinking rider will always take the one in which he can keep his horse straighter and better balanced. The move-off should be clear into working trot and straight down the centre line.

MOVEMENT 2

C	Track to the right.
MRXVK	Medium trot (rising or sitting).
KA	Working trot.

In the turn to the right at the end of the centre line you can very often see the horse bow out slightly just before he turns. This is due to insufficient balance because the rider doesn't keep the horse enough between inside leg and outside rein and doesn't lead into the turn from his outside rein. The medium trot should be well engaged and held consistently from M to K despite the two slight changes of direction. If the horse is off the forehand and well balanced this will be no problem. The transition back to working trot should be clear and submissive.

MOVEMENT 3

A   Continue working trot.
                 From corner: shoulder-in (left).
BXB   Circle to the left 10m diameter.

For comments see under Movement 4.

MOVEMENT 4

BG   Half-pass (left).
GCH   Working trot.

Starting the shoulder-in from the corner allows the rider to get the bend in the turn and continue it into the shoulder-in. The bend should be clear with no tilting of the head and the angle such that the horse strides with its inside hind leg in the direction of its outside foreleg. Engagement and consistency are important. The judge will look for a smooth and balanced transition into the 10m circle which should be continuously round and show the horse well bent in his neck and body. It helps if the rider thinks of riding the circle in two halves. In the half-pass following on from the circle, the horse should maintain the bend and stride forwards/sideways, parallel with the long side, to the marker on the centre line. It is important that the horse reaches the centre line in time to ensure a balanced turn at C. Ideally he should arrive with his shoulder at G and pull himself nicely onto the centre line before turning left. The whole sequence of shoulder-in, 10m circle and half-pass should flow so well into each other that it looks like one movement. One helps to prepare for the other and there is a fundamental link between them.

MOVEMENT 5

HXF   Change rein at extended trot.
FA   Working trot.

There must be a clear transition at H into the extended trot without throwing the horse out of his rhythm. The extension should be in self-carriage and cover as much ground as possible with a bigger frame. A smooth transition back to working trot at F is required so as not to jeopardise the mark for the extended trot.

MOVEMENT 6

A   Halt. Rein-back 5 steps.
                 Proceed at working trot without halting.

Mary Thomson and King William competing at Le Lion d' Angers, France, in 1989.

In this test the halt and rein-back is at A – the furthest place away from the judges, so they will get a clear picture of the overall outline and smoothness of the rein-back and the transitions. The halt should be square and well established at A. The right number of steps is important. The horse should move directly into working trot without stopping.

MOVEMENT 7

A	Continue working trot.
	From corner: shoulder-in (right).
EXE	Circle to the right 10m diameter.

Comments as in Movement 3.

MOVEMENT 8

| EG | Half-pass (right). |
| GCM | Working trot. |

Comments as in Movement 4.

MOVEMENT 9

MXK   Change rein at extended trot.
KA   Working trot.

Comments as in Movement 5.

MOVEMENT 10

AF   Medium walk.
FS   Change rein at extended walk.
SH   Medium walk.

This is the first walk sequence and the horse should settle into a good rhythmical and ground-covering stride. The transitions between medium and extended walk must show a clear difference in length of stride and frame.

MOVEMENT 11

HCR   Working canter.

The transition into working canter is of particular importance, because one mark is given for this movement alone. A clear canter stride should be picked up directly from the medium walk. The horse must stay smooth and steady in the outline. The place for the strike-off, just before the corner, makes it a lot easier for the rider to ensure that the horse picks up the correct canter lead.

MOVEMENT 12

RBEBP   Medium canter (BEB: circle 20m diameter).
PF   Working canter.

Now we have the same movement from the old FEI test, but here it must be performed in medium canter and not medium trot, which I think is easier for the horse's balance and much nicer to ride. Because the horse has a left and right lead in canter he is able to hold a much clearer rhythm on the turn. The judge will mainly look for how balanced the horse stays on the circle and how well the medium stride covers the ground without hurrying. Clear transitions are required and I think the transition back to working canter on the long side is more difficult than the one in trot, because the horse can more easily get crooked to the inside and lose the forward flow.

Richard Walker and Jacana at Badminton in 1991, a few months before winning the team gold and individual silver medals at the European Championships in Punchestown.

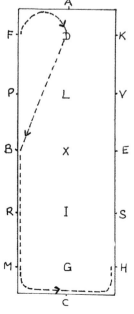

Movement 13.

MOVEMENT 13

FDB   Working canter (FD: half circle 10m diameter).
BRMCH Counter-canter.

For comments see under Movement 14.

MOVEMENT 14

HXF   Change rein at extended canter.
FA   Working canter.

The quality of the last transition is responsible for the next movement. If the horse has resisted coming back at P and not engaged his hind legs underneath his weight, he will lack balance and self-carriage on the 10m half circle and very likely return crooked to the track at B. From a good transition the horse is set up for a more engaged half circle which will automatically give him better balance and rhythm. The horse should be well bent on the line of the half circle, but then return straight from D to B with only a slight flexion remaining in the neck belonging to the right canter. All this should continue into the counter-canter around the short side and there must be no loss of balance, rhythm and fluency on the corners. The balance on the second corner is especially connected with the extended canter. The quality and immediate development of the extension depends upon it. The extended canter should be straight from the corner and cover good ground. The transition at F must be submissive. The fact that the horse returns back to the inside canter will make the rider braver to ask for more extension, but he must be ready for the transition back to medium walk at A for the second walk sequence.

MOVEMENT 15

AK   Medium walk.
KR   Change rein at extended walk.
RM   Medium walk.

This walk is particularly testing of obedience, because the horses are used to staying in canter to the end of the test – a real question of how well the horse is on the rider's aids!

MOVEMENT 16

MCS   Working canter.

Comments as for Movement 11.

MOVEMENT 17

SEBEV   Medium canter (EBE: circle 20m diameter).
VK   Working canter.

Comments as for Movement 12.

MOVEMENT 18

KDE   Working canter (KD: half circle 10m diameter).
ESHCM   Counter-canter.

Comments as for Movement 13.

MOVEMENT 19

MXK   Change rein at extended canter.
KAL   Working canter.

Comments as for Movement 14.

Ginny Leng and Priceless competing in the Los Angeles Olympics.

Movement 20

LG   Working trot.
G   Halt. Immobility. Salute.
      Leave arena at a walk on a long rein at A.

This is exactly the reverse of the old FEI test where horses so easily anticipated the canter strike-off. It does make it easier to control the transition, but the whole mark depends on how settled the horse stays. He should be straight and square in the final halt. As the horse leaves the arena on a long rein the judge can get a last impression of how well and settled the horse has worked in the test.

Collective marks
1. Paces (freedom and regularity).
2. Impulsion (desire to move forward, elasticity of the steps and engagement of the hindquarters).
3. Submission (attention and obedience, lightness and ease of the movements, acceptance of the bridle).
4. Position and seat of the rider, correct use of the aids.

NB: The working, medium and extended trots must be executed 'sitting' unless the term 'rising' is used in the test.

12

THE ROLE OF THE TRAINER

As a trainer one is faced with many different types of pupil and horse; the difficulty lies in making the right assessment and choosing the best method of dealing with their different problems. Variations in temperament and character occur just as much in horses as in people, and the trainer must find a way to deal with both in order to help the horse and rider as a combination.

I feel it is very important for the rider to understand why the trainer is asking him to do a particular thing and how it works, because when a trainer has a limited time with someone, say two or three days, there is only so much he can do. The rider must then be able to follow on what he has learnt in that short time, so he needs to have understood the reasoning behind his trainer's instructions rather than have just done whatever he was asked to do.

Successful training hinges on the trainer's ability to motivate the horse through the rider. The trainer must make the rider understand what is required so that the rider can produce from the horse what the trainer himself would produce if he were riding. If I feel that I cannot influence the horse enough through the rider, I will get on the horse myself and try to make both horse and rider understand what is required and demonstrate what I am talking about. By doing this I can set them both on their way together, though I would prefer to have achieved the right result directly through the rider as this is more satisfying and brings the rider on more quickly. It may be easier for a trainer to get on a horse and make him do what is required, but this doesn't achieve much for the future if the rider has not understood how and why it works.

A trainer has to try to assess a horse's temperament and decide on the best course of action. Some horses might need to be pushed more and dominated; others may need to be handled with more tact. It is not easy to assess a horse fully; he could be difficult because he is anxious and insecure or because he wants to be naughty and go his own way. The right assessment will enable the trainer to approach the problems more effectively.

The trainer also needs to be flexible. Problems that show up in

The most important thing is to make the pupil understand, and this can sometimes involve manual explanations! I could be expressing a demand for more carriage.

a test, such as resistance or difficulty with a particular movement, may have different causes, and the trainer has to feel his way to finding the correct solution. He may try one remedy which doesn't really work, so then he must be prepared to switch to a different policy in order to find the best approach to the problem.

Most event horses are highly strung individuals of largely thoroughbred breeding who find it very difficult to settle in a competition atmosphere. Some are blessed with more movement than others, but the main problem is knowing how to deal with the tension. If most of these horses relaxed and took the leg and hand aids, they could produce quite good and obedient tests; the

It is useful sometimes for the trainer to be able to get on board to demonstrate a point or make a correction if it helps the horse and rider to make progress.

difficulty is that they become lit up by the atmosphere of the competition and then things fall apart.

One of the biggest problems for the trainer is that, although he may get to know the individual horse and rider quite well when working with them at home, he doesn't know how they will react at a competition. That is why I always like to see them in both situations, as things can change quite dramatically; some horses will give you a totally different sort of problem at a competition. When working with a rider at home I like to obtain as much information from him as possible about the horse's behav-

iour and the sort of feel he gets from him at a competition, so that I can decide how the work should be orientated towards that particular situation. However, as it is often difficult to influence the problem directly at home, where it doesn't occur, I also try to give the rider some tips on how to deal with it when competing.

It is important that the rider and trainer devise a system which will work best for each horse when at a competition. Every horse is different, and it is no good trying to force a horse into a certain system just because it works for another. You must be able to adapt and to think of alternative ways of coping with your particular horse's problems.

Different riders need slightly different handling as well. From my experience at international championships and other major competitions, I have found that the trainer has to deal with the temperaments not only of the horses but also of the riders. The importance of the event puts the rider under considerable pressure, and this can affect his performance quite significantly. At the major international events, where the competitors arrive quite early because the horses have had to travel a long way, I have noticed that the horses start off relaxed and working well, but then their tension gradually builds up as the competition draws nearer because the riders themselves are getting hyped-

A training session with Mary Thomson and King William at Badminton during the team concentration in preparation for the Olympic Games in Barcelona. It is important to be able to work closely with the pupil to improve the finer points.

The author taking part in a top-class jumping competition in Germany.

up. There is not a lot the trainer can do at this stage in terms of improving the way a horse is going; he must just concentrate on getting the horse and rider, as a combination, in the best possible frame of mind on the day, when it counts.

INDEX

Page number in *italics* refer to illustrations

Curious George®

WALKS THE PETS

Adapted from the Curious George film series
edited by Margret Rey and Alan J. Shalleck

1 9 8 6

Houghton Mifflin Company Boston

Library of Congress Cataloging-in-Publication Data

Curious George walks the pets.

"Adapted from the Curious George film series."
Summary: George the curious monkey creates chaos when
he tries to take all four of his neighbor's pets for a
walk, especially since they are a dog, cat, canary, and
goldfish.
[1. Monkeys—Fiction. 2. Pets—Fiction] I. Rey,
Margret. II. Shalleck, Alan J. III. Curious George
walks the pets (Motion picture) IV. Title.
PZ7.C92214   1986   [E]   86-7470
ISBN 0-395-39040-0   RNF
ISBN 0-395-39034-6   PAP

Printed in Japan

DNP   10   9   8   7   6   5   4   3   2   1

George was looking out the window.
A neighbor, Mr. Nelson, was walking his dog, Andy.

George was curious.
What would it be like to walk a pet?

Once Mr. Nelson and his dog were back home,
George went over to their house
and rang the doorbell.

Mr. Nelson didn't answer it.
But the door was open, so George went in.

Inside, George discovered Mr. Nelson's other pets.
Besides Andy, he had a cat,

a canary in a cage,

and a goldfish in a bowl.

Could George take *all* of them for a walk?

He tried to put a leash
on the cat, but she ran away.

Next, George opened the birdcage.
But the bird flew away.

The cat jumped after the bird, the bird flew around in circles,
Andy chased the cat, and the goldfish splashed in its bowl.
What excitement!

Suddenly Mr. Nelson rushed in.
"What's going on?" he yelled.

George was scared.
He dropped the leash and ran away.

Mr. Nelson calmed down his pets
and put the bird back in its cage.

After Mr. Nelson left the room,
George came back. He was sure that the pets
would all like to go for a walk.

George had an idea.

After Mr. Nelson left the room,
George came back. He was sure that the pets
would all like to go for a walk.

George had an idea.

He ran back home and got his little red wagon.

He pulled it over to Mr. Nelson's house.

He put the birdcage
and goldfish bowl in the wagon.

Then George hooked the leash
to Andy's collar and tied the other end
to the wagon. Andy could help him pull.

Finally they were ready, and off they went.

Now George was walking all the pets
down the street. Andy pulled the wagon,
and the cat followed behind.

Mrs. James's dog ran out
and trotted behind the cat.
Then Mary O'Brien's cat fell in line, too.

Soon, all the pets in the neighborhood
were following George. What a terrific parade!

But the neighbors didn't think so.
"Stop! Stop!" they shouted angrily.
"What are you doing with our pets? Bring them back!"

George was scared. What could he do now?

"Wait!" called Mrs. James. "Don't be angry.
George can be our pet walker."

"Gee, that's right," said Mary O'Brien.
"George is doing a good job, too," said Mr. Nelson.
"The pets are really behaving now."

"A pet walker will save me a lot of time,"
said Mr. Klein.

Just then, the man with the yellow hat
came running over. "Hold still everybody," he said.
"I want to take your picture. Smile!"